The Prey

By

I0532626

daniel storm

William J. Pulkinen & Associates
705 Sunny Slope Road
Elm Grove, Wisconsin 53122
Pulkinen@wi.rr.com

This book is a work of creativity, observation, research and experience. If any names, events and characters have any resemblance or similarities to actual persons, names, places or events in this story, it is purely coincidental, or the personal knowledge of the author.

ISBN # 9780982678275

Books by: daniel storm

Reaper's Gate

Jury Duty

Praetorian Guard

Surviving the Alphabet Soup

The Apostle

Mantis

The Prey

Not Afraid to Kill, Not Afraid to Die

Masters of the Race

Watch for these titles in Spanish*

Dedication

To whatever power that permits me to rise each day and write, I suppose already knows how much I love to do this and no written thanks are needed.

To those of you who voraciously read my books and question my sanity at the close of each one, I thank you with all my heart.

To the women who manage my career and this literary business I find myself in, thank you. I know I'm tough to manage.

Thus far I have overlooked a special influence in my life, Merlin. You see him as the White Shepard in the photos with me, but for a pup that was so abused and wild when he and I first met, he has been as magical as his namesake. The devotion of a dog is so pure and without regard for their own lives, humans can learn a lot from them. He's part of the family now and king of the castle. Thank you your Majesty for being a part of my life.

Chapter 1

"Oh, you're back with us, huh asshole? Remember me, vato? You still a little groggy?" Evan said as he slapped the man hard across the face.

"Who the fuck are you, Man?"

"My, my, you rob and stab some many defenseless people on buses, you can't take them straight?" Evan said.

"I didn't rob nobody, you old fool. Now let me the fuck outta this thing."

"I told you when you stabbed me, you Spanish shit, that you had no idea who you were fucking with," Evan said and then leaned close to his captive's face. "Well, I survived your knife in my side on the bus that day. Took me a while at the hospital, but I came out of it."

"What, the fuck did you do to me man?"

"Oh, that was GHB. You know the shit you slip in women's drinks so you can get laid because you're too stupid otherwise? I put it in your coffee at the restaurant when you went to take a piss. No one cared or noticed. Hope you don't mind but I'm not a hundred percent yet and it gave me a little edge over you." Evan spat back.

"What you want from me?" You gonna stab me asshole?"

"Oh, heavens no." Evan began and then giggled at the use of the world heavens in his sentence. I've got a real treat for you. Have you figured out who I am yet?"

"Yeah, an asshole who got bitched out of his money by Wrigley Field. I went through your wallet while walking home. You had seventeen bucks, you broke bastard. Seventeen bucks. You some homeless fuck out there?"

No, you just took my lunch money." Evan returned. "You ready to begin your little ride?

"What the fuck you talkin about. Let me outta here. You don't know who you're fucking with?" Evan opened the rear door to the van he had borrowed from the Dodge dealer that was across from the parking lot from where he parked his old car and rolled his Spanish attacker onto the pavement.

"Hey, you can't leave me here, tied up like this!"

"Oh, I wouldn't think of it," Evan began. "We're going for a little drive. I figure about ten miles should do it.

"What are you talking about you crazy bastard? Let me the fuck go and I'll let you live."

Evan, growing tired of the bravado from the little prick who tried to kill him, checked the nylon ropes that held the captive's feet and body. "A little too tight for you, asshole? Does the name Mantis mean anything to you?"

"Yeah, you wanna be like him now. You think you're a killer?"

With a wry smile, Evan leaned very close to the doomed man's face. He could smell the fear on his breath. "I am the Mantis, my little friend, and you are on your way to meeting my Master."

Evan walked back to the cab of the van, turned up Steppenwolf jamming out "Born to be Wild" and started the van's motor. "Get your motor running: Head out on the highway. Looking for adventure," the band sang. You ready for some adventure, asshole?" he asked through the open rear doors.

"Hey man, get back here. I gotta talk to you."

"Time to ride, brother," Evan shouted as he put the van in gear and floored the gas pedal. "Born to be Wild" the music sounded.

"Hey, ouch goddamn it, OK, stop, man. I get the picture. I'll never be an asshole again."

In a few seconds, the van was doing over fifty miles per hour and the man's plea for help turned into screams as the asphalt ground chunks of his flesh from his body. After two miles, the man was silent and Evan noticed he was leaving a blood trail on the road, as he passed under those orange street lamps. The bloody swatch looked as if he had dragged a wet mop behind the van.

After five miles, Evan stopped the van and walked to the rear. What remained tethered to the bumper did not resemble any human form he had ever seen, but it was still breathing. A bloodied something, was rising and falling. The clothes were gone from the knees to the head and the pavement had done its work nicely. "Do you see the Dark Lord yet? You're almost there now."

After driving another five miles while jamming to the rock and roll tunes from an all-night jock, he stopped on an isolated road once again. When he reached the back of the van, he smiled and said, "So, you're with the Master Now." Reaching down to untie the rope holding two bloody and torn legs as they dangle like fuzzy dice from a mirror. Holding the rope only, he dragged the shredded limbs to the side of the road and dropped the rope. Critters would handle the rest of his job tonight. It was time to get back. He had avenged himself and he had spent two nights, fresh out of the hospital where he had lain in a coma for almost a week, locating the Spanish thug that almost dispatched him to hell. He had work to do now.

As he drove, Evan remembered that day on the transit bus, as he watched the cops scouring the fans at Wrigley Field, who had come to watch the White Sox play the Cubs because he, the Mantis, had demanded the Mayor arrange for him. Evan remembered the searing pain as the knife slashed through his flesh and organs, just before he blacked out.

When he awoke in the pale blue room of the hospital, he remembered the gentle voice of a nurse named Florence. She had been very kind and attentive to his every need, bringing him water, soda, food and bathing him in the bed with hot towels. When she had informed him that the police wanted to know when they could ask him about his attacker, he knew that he could not allow any such meeting to happen and on the second-shift, he dressed in the freshly laundered clothes he was wearing when stabbed on the bus and blended in with the visitors leaving the hospital. He was no longer "John Doe" in the hospital. He was the Mantis, once again.

Finding his attacker had been easier than he had imagined those nights as he lay in bed, anticipating the day when he could resume his true being on this earth as the most prolific and feared serial killer to ever live and die. Seems the man who knifed him on his glorious day, had a local reputation as a tough, Riding the bus and telling elderly passengers about his near death experience, gleaned the local haunts for the man who believed he was invincible. After spotting him in a greasy-spoon diner, he doubted the moron would recognize him and actually sat in the booth across from him. When the tattooed freak went to the bathroom, Evan dropped three of the sleeping pills Florence had asked him to take and get some rest, into his coffee cup. When the man returned, he had the waitress top it off with hot brew and added enough sugar to sweeten the Chicago Bears defense.

In the parking lot, dazed as if he had been tackled by Brian Urlacher of the Bears, it was simple for Evan to glide the wobbling cretin to the van, Seated in the back, Evan began binding him like a mummy, with row after row of yellow nylon rope, which almost coated his upper torso when tied off. Tying the feet was reminiscent of when he has suspended his "offerings" above the floor of his workshop, before rendering them like a hog at market.

Secure now, Evan laid the witless felon in the back of the cargo area and began driving. He knew of the perfect road where the kids drag race their hot rod exotics and is seldom patrolled by police. Once he reached that spot, he confronted the man that thought he could kill the Mantis.

Leaving the van out front of the Dodge dealer, the rear doors spattered with bloody chunks of flesh, Evan laughed aloud. "You have no idea what this van is really worth now," Evan explained to the name above the dealership. "If you only knew," he said, as he just walked off in to the night.

His side ached all the time, despite the staples and the stitches being removed the day he left the hospital and yet he had not had any cranial pain from the tumor that was in the very core of his brain and well on his way to killing him. He thanked the Dark Lord for sparing him that suffering, on top of the healing process going on inside of him. Pain was an old friend of Evan's. The Dark Lord shielded him from the most heinous pain and in exchange, he would do the master's work.

Thus far, Evan Felder, the insurance administrator from Wheaton, Illinois, had set the media work on fire, after being dubbed "the Mantis" when he left the skeletal remains in front of a museum. Since, that time, the world begged news of the Mantis and his homicidal exploits, daily. International media carried stories of his sanctifications and offerings, created from the bones of homosexuals, whom he had arranged eternal life with the Dark

Lord. All one had to do was read the manifesto Evan had crafted and delivered to a local media slut who would trade his soul for a position in Washington or as an anchorman for the major network show.

It was time to let the world know that the Mantis was back and moving to the next level. National.

Chapter 2

The Belle of the Homicide Division of the Chicago Police Department, Sgt. Rachael Hart, is by far the most notable cop on the force. Her staunch Irish heritage, red hair, fair skin and ocean of freckles, is worn like a badge of courage or honor. Her fame, stemming from several nationally publicized arrests of murderers, has cast her into the spotlight of media hounds and wherever she goes, someone mentions her service to the law enforcement community or thanks her for making the streets of Chicago a little safer.

Benedict Ori, the Chief of Homicide, recruited her from Evanston Police, a northern suburb of Chicago, after working with her on a murder. The lumbering giant, whose soft-spoken words are received like the voice of God to Moses, considers this Irish girl as family, he and his wife never had. Throughout the Homicide Division, it is well settled that Rachael is the heir –apparent to Ben when he retires and she has earned the respect of those she works with, through loyalty, honor and courage in the field.

As a judo instructor and competitor in the national events, she has presented herself as a worthy opponent or partner in a fight. Only certain members of the Department are privy to her achievements on the shooting range, where she qualified as "expert" in handguns and rifles. Her steady hand and eye coordination were a gift from human clay.

The male members of the Department know that Rachael is "unavailable," some of whom learned the hard way after landing on their backsides, as she is hopelessly in love with a man named Daniel Salvino, who is an international warrior in martial arts competitions and considered as one of the most lethal men on this planet by experts to the combative world. Little is known about his livelihood, however, as he declines to discuss financial matters with anyone. Together, when attending gala affairs within and without the Department, they make a fantastic couple.

"Ben, it's been weeks since the crap with the base-ball game at Wrigley Field." Rachael said, as she sipped her coffee while sitting in her boss's office.

"What's your point? You want this guy to kill again?" Ben asked.

"Of course not! I think this guy is moving. I think he's packed up here, wherever 'here' was, and is taking his show on the road," she returned.

"Rachael," Ben began, while setting his pen down and picking up his own coffee cup now. "The FBI believes that our Mantis character has gone to ground and is keeping his head down. I don't believe a lot of that, as this psychotic cretin believes he's invincible, but I do think he's smart enough to find ways to stay under the radar."

"I think this guy needs more attention. He feeds on the media and press. That's why he wrote that stupid Manifesto of his. It was all bullshit, Ben, Just another way to get attention. I think he feels he is no longer fit for this pond and is headed for the ocean," she replied.

"Hmmmm," Ben began, as he sipped hot coffee. "I am convinced this guy wants more attention, but he has a comfortable zone here someplace and I'm not convinced he'll abandon it."

"If all that analysis stuff from the BAU in Quantico is believable, then it fits that our killer will move on." She replied.

The Behavioral Analysis Unit of the Federal Bureau of Investigation, which is housed in Quantico, Virginia, at the headquarters of the lead federal law enforcement agency. Given the assignment to study psychological profiles obtained from some of America's most profound killers were recorded, the BAU is a valuable resource in the fight to reduce violent crime and capture those who are driven to murder innocents. By pinpointing traits and psychological nuances, the BAU provides a unique snapshot of a perpetrator's likely habits and haunts, giving field agents a narrower focus.

"Well, Dr. Hart, I am all ears. Please give me your interpretation of our killer's profile." Ben said, as he leaned back in his chair and folded his mighty hands across his belly.

"Before you make fun of this, listen. I can feel this guy's presence, Ben. So can the people. Sort of like when a shark is in the area, all the little fish know and scurry around. The people aren't scared right now. He's not around, Ben." Rachael sat back in her chair, waiting for Ben to react, but he was just watching her.

"And you want me to authorize an alert to several surrounding states because the fish aren't scared?" Ben asked calmly.

"No. Just Wisconsin for now. Its close, will give him fresh waters to hunt and it's rural enough to afford him places to hide.

"Just Wisconsin, not Indiana, which is minutes south of here." Ben enquired.

"Not rural. He needs the country to hide in."

"OK, I'll authorize Wisconsin, Rachael. I learned to follow my instincts years' ago and look where it got me?"

I'm not trying for a desk job, Ben. I'm a street cop. Period," she answered.

"No, I'm not talking about the desk, Rachael. I'm talking about the old, fat, alive and training the sexiest Homicide Chief Chicago will ever see." He returned and they began to laugh.

By the time Melvin Gibson, aka "Hollywood," due to some of the hijinx associated with his arrests he has made in his career with the FBI, along with his partner Khoren Perzigian, the rational side to this dynamic duo, arrived at C.P.D. headquarters, Rachael had prepared the official alert that would be sent to all Wisconsin law enforcement in Wisconsin. She carried it into the meeting in Ben's office, where they were awaiting her arrival.

"Hi Rachael," Gibson said as she entered. Both of them remembered the time where they were almost mortal enemies and combative. More than once, she had twisted one of his arms and in return, he had dropped her on her ass on the sidewalk. Since that time, they have learned that each other has the same goal. "Catching the Mantis." Whether the Mantis wants to be captured or shoot it out right then, both of them are prepared to grant him his wish.

Khoren Perzigian, on the flipside, is quite and constrained. At least, when compared to Gibson. He's a family man, unlike Gibson, and cherishes his kids. When Gibson destroyed a multi-million dollar home with a half-million dollar powerboat, belonging to a certain quarterback from the New England Patriots, which they were commended for later, Khoren followed his partner to the Windy City. Of Armenian descent, he has an olive hued flesh tone, giving him the permanent suntan look. Slightly overweight, people often think he is lethargic and snail-like. However, he trains in the FBI gym and eats a hearty meal afterword, negating the calorie burning session before hand.

"Nice of you to come here, Mr. FBI." Rachael began taunting him. "Please excuse the appearance. Our decorator had the carpeting removed, while the painters are here."

"I thought there was some reason why the place looked more like a homeless shelter than a professional office." He returned.

"The FBI is here to help, Rachael, not give us new lines for comedy stints. Right Mr. Gibson," Ben said.

"Ah, yes sir, we're here to help you serve and protect." He replied.

"Well then, what wisdom do you bring us, Mr. FBI?" she said.

"We've given up following the kid from Office Cheapo, as he was fired and moved to his father's place in another state. I don't think the Mantis entertains the thought of him as a victim. Too messy." Gibson said, and then continued. "We think he's hunkered down and trying to avoid capture. We're getting too close to him."

"You make it sound like we have his name and address," she quipped.

"Not yet Sergeant," Khoren interrupted," but our guys are working on that. No one can be that invisible. We'll have a match soon."

"And in the meantime?" Ben asked now.

"Well, Sir, we have identified areas in and close to Chicago, where he is most likely to hide" Khoren said.

"But he's not here anymore," Rachael exclaimed.

"Oh? Did you have a chat with him about his travel plans? Care to share?" Gibson mused.

"Rachael says the fish aren't scared, so he isn't around here," Ben said now.

"What? Fish aren't scared? Rachael, have you taken too many headshots fighting? What the hell do the fish have to do with the Mantis?" Gibson asked.

"Thanks, Ben. I appreciate that. I really do, "she said to her boss.

"Rachael says our killer is like a shark and the people know when they're in danger. Like fish when a shark is near," Ben responded now.

"And you are an expert in fish now?" Gibson asked.

"Listen, you federal twit. You're in your ivory tower there on Dearborn, while I work the streets and alleys of Chicago. The people, you nose picker, can sense danger. Ask any Chicagoan. If this guy were near, they'd be indoors, safe, not in the parks or at the beaches. They don't sense the danger" she fired back.

"So, you see people in the park and that means the Mantis left town," Khoren said now.

"It's hard to explain, but people in Chicago know when to close their doors and windows, or keep their kids home from school. It's intuition. People aren't afraid and that means something here."

"I have to agree with her, gentlemen. I've been a cop a long time and my instincts have solved more cases than your BAU or fancy crime scene techniques. I think she may be right." Ben said.

"So, where do you think our killer ran off to?" Gibson asked with a slight grin on his face.

"I'm betting on Wisconsin. It gives him cover and a fresh start," she responded.

Looking to Ben now, Gibson asked, "And you're cosigning this, Ben? You believe what she says?"

"I think a cop has to follow their instincts. I believe in Rachael and her instincts. So, yes, I am cosigning it," Ben said proudly.

"OK, we'll notify our offices up there. We won't say anything about fish though. We'll call it 'deductive reasoning' that leads us to conclude that the killer has relocated. OK?" Khoren said, while Gibson sat looking at the floor and shaking his head.

"You have something to say Agent Gibson?" Ben asked.

"Your fish had better be right, Rachael, or we're letting a shark hunt while we're chasing red herring."

"The people know these things. You haven't been here long enough to see yet," she returned.

"If you're wrong, I won't be around here long enough to test that theory, either. OK, we're all on-board then. We believe the Mantis is now a cheese head. Let's see what he does now." Gibson said as he stood up to leave.

"I didn't mean the 'nose picker' part if its any consolation to you," Rachael said with a smile.

Rachael, I've been called worse in official memos too, so don't worry about that," he replied, then added "And I've never picked my nose where anyone could see me."

"You're disgusting," Rachael said, laughing. "Don't you fibbies ever work?"

"Sure we do, Sergeant. We're the ones that tore up your carpeting, Khoren interjected.

"so, we're all on the same page here?" Ben asked as everyone rose from their seats.

Turning to Rachael, Gibson said, "Your freckles better be right, Irish, or we're kissing the Blarney stone soon."

"I'm right," Rachael answered.

"OK then, it's settled. We focus on Wisconsin now," Gibson said before shaking hands and leaving.

After the FBI men left, Ben said, "I hope your freckles are right too. If not, we'll be emptying parking meters in front of City Hall."

"Thanks for backing me up, Ben. I'm right, though, our bug has flown elsewhere."

Chapter 3

"Associated Press. How may I help you?" the female voice said.

"I want to speak with your Chief in Chicago," Evan demanded.

"That would be Mr. Medrano, sir. Can I have your number so he can call you?" the voice asked sweetly.

"No, I said I want to speak to him, not leave a goddamn message." Evan responded caustically, as he looked at his fingernails. He swore to himself that he had trimmed his nails just two days ago, but given their length, he began to question the veracity of that notion.

"You needn't curse at me sir. Let me see if Mr. Medrano is accepting calls."

"What do you mean 'accepting calls'? Of course he's accepting calls. It's what you people do," Evan replied.

"Please hold," was all Evan heard before "elevator" music blurted into his delicate ears.

While rinsing his face, Evan noticed how bloodshot his eyes were and vowed to himself to get more rest. He told himself to drink less coffee, as it was keeping him awake, evidently and staining his teeth as well, which he noticed, a yellow patina dulling his teeth to lemon yellow. He scrubbed his teeth with toothpaste for almost ten minutes, foam pouring from his mouth, but his teeth remained stained. Being the Mantis, he realized, was quite a job and his body seemed to be paying a heavy price. However, Evan knew the Dark Lord was watching over him.

"Mr. Medrano wants to know what this call is in reference to," the female voice said when back on the line.

"Ask Mister Medrano if he would like to talk to the Mantis. In thirty seconds, I will hang up and call UPI, understood girlie?" Evans replied.

"Yes sir, you're the third Mantis today."

"Perhaps, sweet cakes, but I'm the real real," Evan said suavely.

"Hold on, Hollywood. I'll relay your deal message."

The elevator music began and Evan focused on the second hand of his watch. In exactly eight seconds, he would disconnect..."This is Sergio Medrano. With whom am I speaking?"

"Despite the crackpots calling you claiming to be me, I am the guy you people call the Mantis" Evan said matter-of-factly.

"Well, nice to meet you Mr. Mantis. How do I know you're you?" Sergio said.

"How would you like me to leave a body at your office? Or, perhaps just some parts of me?"

"You needn't harm anyone on our part, sir, We just report the news." Sergio returned.

"Well then, how would you like to verify who I am?"

"How about you tell me something only the Mantis could know? Something, that wasn't reported in the news," Sergio said.

"I soaked them in muriatic acid before I dropped them off." Evan said quickly.

As the station chief in Chicago, Sergio was privy to the plethora of investigative reports that were gathered by reporters in the field. Although the AP never reported the minor detail of the acid wash, he was keenly aware of the truth of that statement.

"What can I do for you, Mr. Mantis?" Sergio asked.

"How would you like exclusive access to me for interviews and such? You get the exclusive, directly from me and not some reporter." Evan taunted.

"And what you want in return, Mr. Mantis?"

"Two hundred-fifty thousand bucks, you have exclusive access to me for updates, news and interviews," he responded.

"Well, I don't have the authority to give away a quarter a million dollars, Mr. Mantis."

"Bullshit, you have the power to sign off on that and we both know it. Do you want me to make the same offer to UPI?" Evan snarled.

"How do I know you wouldn't take the money and not live up to your side of the deal? After all, sir, if you are who you claim to be, you're a notorious criminal?" Sergio responded.

"You don't, Mr. Station Chief, however just one interview with me will bring the AP ten times what you're going to pay me.

The truth in the last statement was evident, but what the caller failed to comprehend, was that Sergio sought the laurels associated with a Pulitzer Prize or even the Nobel Prize, if he could garner them. Without question, he realized the value of contact with such a killer.

"And if I agree, how do you propose to meet and exchange?" Sergio enquired, with a guarded tone.

"How long will it take you to get the money?"

"A couple of hours at least. I have to get his approval and have security go with me to the bank."

"Leave your security people at the office, Boss Hoss, when you come to meet me, or I leave. Goes for the cops, too, so don't blow it. Understand?" Evan asked.

"Yes, yes I understand. How will I get in touch with you Mr. Mantis? Ah...what do I call you, besides Mr. Mantis?"

"Quentin. I'll call you back in three hours, so you should be ready. At that time, I'll tell you how we meet. Understand?" Evan asked.

"Three hours. I'd better get going then. Quentin," he added at the end.

Click. End of conversation.

Sergio Medrano began with the Associated Press in his home country, Mexico, where he clawed his way to the top of the media ranks through hard work and an eye for a story. When he was offered the Chicago office, he snapped up the offer and packed his family up. A citizen now, he enjoys the freedoms all citizens maintain and he respects the laws of his new country, but when the proverbial "once in a lifetime" stories come your way, you have to be prepared to risk it all or lose your turn.

After setting the phone down, Sergio called his secretary to have her call the national office in New York. He needed approval for quarter-million dollar expenditure, although he could approve it himself. Risk was acceptable, only in moderation.

While Sergio explained to his boss in New York that he was "investing "the funds in a story that would reap millions in return," the bank was assembling the money.

Across town, Evan Felder sat in his car, the ideas that come with winning the lottery, dancing through his head. He had never held such a large sum of cash in his hands at one time and could almost feel the power that money brings. He decided it was time for a new car. Not brand new, the thought, but something fresher. "Would look good driving along with a couple offerings inside and the old car quits running," he said to himself, then giggled as he envisioned a headline; "Mantis captured when clunker breaks down." And so it was ordained that the Mantis would be shopping for a new car, or truck, or SUV. Precisely three hours later, Sergio's phone rang.

"Medrano"

"Sir, there's a Quentin that says you're expecting his call," the operator said.

"Put him through, please."

When Sergio heard the connection made he said, Sergio Medrano. Can I help you?"

"You got the money, Mr. Station Chief?"

"Yes, it just arrived. Good thing you didn't hold me to two hours after all," he replied nervously.

"Good. What are you wearing?" Evan said and then remembered the standard blue business suit that all execs wore. "Never mind. Put a yellow flower in your lapel and come out of your building, then turn right. I'll be behind you, unless I see anything suspicious. If that happens, Sergio, you will be my next offering in a cardboard box. Got that?"

Sergio hadn't considered that the Mantis may be him and the thought send chills down his back, while his office suddenly became hot to him.

"Give me time to find a flower. I don't know if we have anything like that," he replied.

"Sure, take your time. In ten minutes you walk out the front door alone, except for my money, or I walk away." Evan said.

"Ten minutes. I got that." Sergio replied. Click.

Looking around the office for a yellow flower, he spotted an artificial arrangement with yellow roses made of silk. Grabbing one of the flowers, he tried to break the stem so it would look correct then realized it was made of wire and gave up. He quickly pushed the end of the green wire through the button-hole on his lapel and tried to calm himself.

With his life a Pulitzer Prize riding on how it would all transpire, Sergio arrived in the lobby, with a long green wire dangling in front of his blue suit coat, while carrying a gym bag with the cash that would make him a sensation.

As soon as he exited the building on W. Wacker, he looked at the sea of faces that surrounded him. Anyone of those faces could be the most prolific killers America had ever bread.

"Hola, Sergio! Don't turn around. Let's turn right shall we?" Evan said from behind. Evan had been waiting in the lobby of the building, when Sergio rushed past.

"OK, Where we going, Quentin?" he said nervously now.

"We're going to catch a cab, Boss. Get to know each other." Evan replied. "This one will do just fine right here. Let's grab it."

Sergio slapped the top of the cab lightly, and then opened the door. "You got a fare?"

"Sure, I loaded. Can't you see? The hack driver said sarcastically.

Sergio slid into the rear seat and looked at Evan, who had slid in beside him.

"Where to?" the cabbie asked.

"Museum of Natural History, please," Evan said.

"Sure thing. Hell, you're my biggest fare all friggin day. You're about six blocks away or so."

"Please, just drive," Sergio returned, then looked at the man next to him.

Dressed in rumpled slacks and pullover, no-name shirt, his hair slightly disheveled, bloodshot eyes, yellow teeth and hard scrabbled ears, Evan was either a fashion-ista or homeless. Sergio couldn't determine which.

"Is that mine, Mr. Station Chief?" Evan asked. Without a word, as if Hollywood cameras were rolling, Sergio pushed the gym bag across the seat.

"Great. Now your wallet, please." Evan commanded.

"You're robbing me?"

"Just slide it over, Mr. Medrano. Let's not make a scene. Someone may hear you."

Reluctantly, Sergio withdrew his wallet from inside his suit coat and slid it over.

With wrinkled hands as if they hadn't been trimmed in weeks, his wallet was lifted and opened.

Removing Sergio's driver's license, which he slid into the front pocket of his slacks. Evan slid the wallet back to Sergio.

"What do you want that for? You'll never pass as me?" Sergio inquired.

"If anything goes wrong, Boss, I know where to find you and your family." Evan said coldly.

The thought of the Mantis knowing where he and his family resided, sent a shockwave of fear through him. He thought to himself, "What have I done?"

"Relax. It's just insurance. We're business partners now. You're the safest man in America. Anyone bothers you and they deal with me." Evan boosted.

"So, Sergio began with a slight stutter to his voice, "tell me a little about you. Quentin."

"We'll have plenty of time for that later. First, I want you to know that I am branching out. Sort of like a franchise." Evan said.

"You mean you have helpers?"

"No, you moron, I'm giving you national news. Chicago is just one city my Master wants to show his presence in. Now I expand." Evan replied as he looked out the cab window and recognized the vary office building he worked at a million years ago.

"Can we interview you before you leave? I'm sure you want your story memorialized, right? In case something happens?"

"You mean like if I get killed somehow, right?" Evan snarled back.

"Well, there's always that possibility in your line of work, that is."

"Yes, you'll get an interview," Evans replied after he considered the request.

"Good. Let's walk and talk? I'll listen, mostly and you can tell me whatever comes to mind. OK?"

"Give me your phone."

"What? Why…"

"Give –me-your-phone. Now!" Evan demanded.

Sergio slid the Apple I-Phone 4 out of his right suit pocket and slid it over. A flashing red light told Evan that the recording application was engaged and Sergio had been recording every word.

"Strike one, Mr. Station Chief. You do not want to get to strike two, or someone close to you will end up in a cardboard box with only a face left. Am I clear?"

Yes. Very. My boss told me to record you, so we had proof we didn't have a role in anything that you've done or doing. I'm sorry."

"Well, it cost you the only strike that doesn't come with consequences. Understand?" Evan asked.

"Yeah, I understand."

Adroitly, Evan dismantled the expensive phone and dropped the pieces into the gym bag.

"Here you are big spenders. That'll be seven-fifty." The cabby shouted while looking in the mirror.

"Pay the man, boss. You're writing this off on taxes anyhow."

With a slight hesitation while contemplating a snappy reply and thinking better of it, Sergio handed the driver a ten-dollar bill. "Keep the change."

"Oh, a big tipper too. You gotta be royalty" the driver said as he waited for Sergio to exit his cab before rejoining the endless ebb and flow of yellow cabs everywhere.

"Now what, Quentin?"

"Nothing. I leave here and make headlines. You go back to your office, get a new phone and driver's license and wait for my call." Evan replied.

"That's it? A quarter of a million dollars for a cab ride?" Sergio said ingratiated.

"Relax, Boss Man. You'll get your Pulitzer Prize off me. I'm going to make you as famous as that spic, Geraldo Rivera."

"My boss is going to have my head. I just gave a way two hundred fifty kay on a cab ride."

"Relax, Boss. You want something for your cash now?" Evan asked.

"that would help, Quentin. A lot."

"OK, here's one the cops don't even know I did. There's this fat cow named Maglio who was stealing shit from people's houses she was inspecting. I killed the bitch with a concrete frog, and then burned the place to make it look good. Got that?"

How do you spell 'Mah-lio'? M-a-g-l-i-o, was on her mailbox." Evan responded.

"When will we talk again? Will we meet in person each time?" Sergio asked.

"We'll see. I don't know that I want you recording everything like that."

"I promise not to record without telling you first," Sergio replied.

"Good. You're starting to get the hang of this Mr. Station Chief. You never want to see me angry."

"No, I suppose not. Answer me one question before you leave?"

"Be quick about it. I have a plane to catch "Evans said back.

"Why do you deliver just bones? What does that mean to you?" Sergio asked the killer.

"The Dark Lord welcomes these people into his kingdom in their purest form. I just arrange the meeting, Mr. Station Chief." Evan said proudly.

"The Dark Lord? You mean Satan?"

"The Master is referred to by several names. The Bible calls him a serpent and Satan. You must be a Christian, Mr. Boss."

"Catholic actually. So, you serve this Dark Lord, do you? He commands these killings?" Sergio asked meticulously.

"The Master controls all of us, Mr. Station Chief. He's inside everyone. All I do is harvest the sinners who offend him."

"Can I quote you on that, Quentin?" Sergio asked.

"You paid for it, Mr. Boss Man. Do with it as you please. I have to go now. I'll be in touch." Evan said before hailing another cab and leaving.

Sergio Medrano could hardly contain the excitement that rushed through his veins. This would be the biggest story of his career, but, as his boss had advised him earlier, every word of it would have to pass muster with corporate counsel prior to any release.

When Sergio and the Associated Press finally released the story, the world clamored for more and the money rolled into the AP coffers like rain water to the Mississippi.

What Sergio Medrano was not prepared for, although the switchboard was inundated with requests for him to appear on just about every network news talk-show in the country, the sudden appearance of Rachael Hart and the FBI agents Gibson and Perzigian.

Even in the blue windbreaker with FBI on the front and back, Sergio felt testosterone surge at the sight of her.

"May I help you?" Sergio said, wounding hurt as the intrudes barged into his office, a secretary in tow telling them "you can't go in there."

"Yeah, you can and will help us, or you're leaving here in cuffs," Rachael said, dangling handcuffs in front of her.

"That does not scare me, officer. I have a right to free press."

"You'll get to argue that at trial. For now, you've got an appointment down the street. Gibson said.

"With or without handcuffs, Mr. Medrano?" Rachael asked.

"I am not running anywhere. I have no reason to. I report the news, that's all."

"C'mon Clark Kent," Gibson said, getting behind Sergio as he walked out of his office.

"Call counsel and let them know they were right,"

Sergio said to a secretary. "They'll know what to do."

Chapter 4

Armed with the cash received from the Associated Press, Evan prepares for his migration north, to the virgin territory of Wisconsin. Soon the "cheese "state would become the fresh hunting grounds for the man they had only heard about.

Interstate 94, although eight lanes wide, is a trip through the country, as it winds its way past the major cities along the way. "Welcome to Wisconsin," Evan said to himself as he entered the state on its southern edge. He loved looking at the fields of tall corn, their tassels swaying with the breeze. The smell of country air made him smile and more relaxed. Leaving the hustle and bustle of Chicago life was welcomed and the thought of serving the Dark Lord in such a seemingly vulnerable state, was intoxicating.

Since leaving Chicago, he was fixated on looking at himself quite often in the rearview mirror, He was different somehow, yet he couldn't place it. Sure his eyes were bloodshot, but he hadn't been sleeping in five star hotels lately, instead grabbing an hour here and there in the car, so the red eyes were to be expected. His face, somehow, looked paler but he thought that was due to the contrast with his eyes. He told himself that he needed a couple days rest, before he could resume his role as the Mantis.

Spotting the huge auto mall adjoining the highway, with every manufacturer being represented in a separate section, Evan decided to do a little shopping. The used car lot had about a thousand vehicles at least and he began narrowing down the numbers. A car, such as the one he was currently using lacked versatility and space. "Trucks and SUV's," the sign read and Evan headed that way. Then, he had to make a decision regarding the ample space of a pick-up truck versus an SUV. The open bed of the pick-up is useful for transporting offerings to the master, but impractical when attempting to hide the bodies from nosey truckers, cops and those in buses. So, he ambled over to the lines of SUV's. The first vehicle he encountered is an emerald green Jeep Grand Cherokee, where it sat on an elevated turn style.

"She is a beauty, isn't she," he heard from behind.

"Huh?" Evan responded.

"The Jeep, Sir. She's the nicest we have on the lot. Every option you can imagine and low miles too. Hi, my name's George Ruth, but people call me Babe, after the baseball player," the salesman said as he extended his hand to Evan.

Without shaking the man's hand, he didn't want the salesman to see how long his fingernails were, Evan said, "Can I see inside?"

"Sure, let me get the keys to pull it off. May I have your driver's license, sir, so I can make a copy before we take'er out? Insurance stuff." He added at the very end.

"I'm not sure I want to drive it yet. May I see the inside now?"

The old trick of making a photocopy of the driver's license, "for insurance purposes," where the names and addresses were cultivated by sales reps and entered into data systems for flyers announcing sales events, failed on Evan and the sales man trudged off to the sales office to retrieve the keys.

"Rachael would love you," Evan said as he gnarled hand slid over the highly polished surface.

His hands! That's when he noticed the long, yellowish nails, the wrinkled flesh just starting to form on the backs and the slight curvature of his fingers, which he attributed to driving, lack of sleep and no exercise.

Evan did not want to waste any more time with the salesman, especially listening to his spiel about free car washed for life and the "first oil change is on us," so he asked the man what he would take for the Jeep.

"It's only a year old, sir, and in mint condition...," was all the salesman got out before Evan interrupted him.

"I don't care about your car washes and oil changes you imbecile. Do you want to sell the thing or make it fit up your ass?" Evan asked, shocking the man.

"Sir, there is no need to be nasty. Of course I would like to sell you the vehicle, but not if you're going to insult me."

"How would you like to look at your balls, as you hold them in your hand?"

The salesman decided to avoid further conflict with Evan, which probably saved his life. "Would it be a financed deal?"

"I'll take off three thousand dollars. No trade and no financing." The salesman said.

"Deal. I'll need to leave my car here a few days till I can come back for it. That OK with you?"

"I don't see a problem. Are you titling in this state or another. I'll take care of that when I get back to Illinois," Evan stated.

"Fine, sir. Let's go inside and write this up. Can I get your coffee or something?"

"Sure, I'd like some James Earl Ray Tea, with a sliver of fresh lemon and two cubes of sugar."

"Excuse me? I don't think we have anything like that James Earl Ray stuff."

"Gray, you moron. James Earl Ray was a killer, not a tea!" Evan said, feigning disgust.

"I'm sorry, sir. Is there anything else I can get you?" the salesman asked.

"Yes, outta here in the Jeep, before I have the urge to taste forbidden fruit."

"Ah, yes sir, fruit. We don't have fruit either. Let me get started on the paperwork. Do you need to call your bank for the transfer, sir?"

"That's not necessary, but thanks for the offer to use your phone. Now, can I get the hell outta here?" Evan asked.

"We can't accept an out of state check, sir," he said back.

"Did I say I was giving you a check? I said cash. Now, I am leaving here in ten minutes, with or without the Jeep. Your choice." Evan shot back.

"What name is going on this, sir?"

"George Washington. Does it make a difference?" Evan enquired.

Now, the salesman wanted this whack-job out of his office and as far away as the full tank of gas in the Jeep could carry him. "No sir. I'll have it ready in a minute."

Evan was the proud owner of an emerald green Jeep and on his way toward Milwaukee, after he parked his Taurus in the rear of the "Service department and transferred his personal effects to the Jeep's ample space. The jeep even smelled new and rode like the luxury SUV that it was intended to be.

With the windows open and sun roof fully retracted, the experience was nothing short of exquisite. The sun shone through the open top, while the wind whipped around the interior. Surely, the Dark Lord was pleased with him, as he was almost pain free.

The exit sign read "Racine," but to Evan, he saw the Motel 6 sign and decided it was time for some well-deserved rest and a hot shower. He would look and feel better, after some peace and quiet.

When Evan laid the money on the counter, the clerk no longer cared about the photo ID or credit card for the charges. A three hundred dollar deposit was all she needed. He signed in under Jame Shu and got a little laugh from the clerk, as she caught the hidden joke as well. "Have a nice night, Mr. Shu. With the missus be joining you later?" she asked coyly.

"Perhaps." Evan said, playing along.

"Would you like an extra key, sir?"

"No thanks. I'll let her in," Evan said over his shoulder as he walked out the lobby doors.

Evan's next stop was for clothing and toiletries and he headed east on highway 11, where he came upon a store called "Fleet-Farm" and decided to stop.

To Evan's delight, the store had everything he would need, including clothing, household items and even tools for the handyman. Evan made a mental note to come back to the store for all his handyman needs.

With new blue jeans, plaid Carhart shirt, work boots and toiletries, he headed back towards the motel, but his hunger took control of him now, so he headed for town and a hot meal. Still in the rural part of the Racine County area, Evan noticed an empty lot with what could only be an abandoned gas station. The lot was surrounded with a chain link fencing, with rusted gates out front. Weeds grew through cracks in the asphalt parking lot and were almost two feet in height. Evan drove into the lot and parked.

Wiping dust from the windows with his hand, Evan could see the barren interior.

Every piece of usable equipment had been moved out. All that remained was the ancient hydraulic floor lift. This building showed promise as the next workshop for the Mantis.

On the frontage road, where Evan sought the breakfast menu of a Bob Evans, which Evan found quite amazing in namesake, he passed a small airport. Cautiously, Evan drove into the parking lot. The airport was small, but handled an array of aircraft, from gliders to twin engine. Without having an explanation, the rusted hanger at the end of the row beckoned him. The door was unlocked and partially opened, so Evan stepped in.

The hanger was obviously unused, as a few boxes of junk were strewn about the dusty floor. A single overhead lap and mechanical chain hoist told him he had discovered the Mantis' new lair. He would have to change the door lock, but otherwise, the hanger was remote enough and would permit him to park the Jeep inside while he worked.

"Perfect, Master. I shall make it mine." Evan said to the floor.

After having a hearty breakfast, in the middle of the afternoon, Evan was ready for some sleep time. The hot shower, where he trimmed his finger and toenails, whatever strength that permitted Evan to function, was sapped from his body and he collapsed on the bed. Immediately, he fell asleep and was visiting the empire of the Dark Lord, where children played in the lush green meadows and the inhabitants wore fine silk garments as they sang and joked in the streets. It is a glorious place, this land where he dispatches his offerings to. He looked for familiar faced, but saw none. He knew they were there and happy that Evan had chosen them for eternal life with the Master.

It was dark when Evan awoke. Pain was building in his head and he recognized it as a signal from the Dark Lord that an offering would soon be needed.

"As you will, Master," Evan said as he held his head between both hands and stared at the stained carpet on the floor. "As you will." Soon.

Chapter 5

The Bible speaks clearly on the powers the Dark Lord or Satan possesses. To a human, even the tiniest fragment of those powers, smaller than any electron microscope can detect that mortal will feel invincible. Although unable to fly like comic book characters, those blessed by the Master of All Things Unholy, would exhibit greater abilities in alternate areas.

For example, Evan Felder can identify men who have chosen the "alternative lifestyle" of having men as their lovers. The term homosexual is the diagnostic term but Evan has all of the slang terms reserved for his references to such men.

Returning to Fleet-Farm for his "tools," which he has carefully been selecting for over an hour now, he spotted and identified a young man in the next isle as "a queer." It did not require the omnipotent powers of the Dark Lord to realize this guy was cut from an alternative fabric. John "Penis Head" Wade, as his friends call him, has more metallic piercings in his flesh than contestants on Ripley's shows. His lips, nose, eyebrows and ears are the ones visible and the imagination is not stretched too far to encompass the other areas of his body, Wade was violated with stainless steel.

It does not require a Disney artist to describe the male body parts Wade's head is fashioned after and hence, the Penis Head moniker. It did not require Dr. Ruth to explain Wade's sexual preferences either, especially when he was holding hands with a man that was not only the "man" of the relationship, but also twice Wade's age.

Being the "bitch," Wade would service his man, obviously, which sent a torrent of hatred running through Evan's psyche. A woman will drain the seminal canal, as it is ordained by the Bible, as it was Adam and Eve, not Adam and Steve. Evan has waged a private war on such defiled creatures and given them unto his Master, as Penis Head is soon to be.

Without purchasing a single item, much to the dismay of the store security who thought he might be shoplifting, Evan left the store and waited in his Jeep for Wade and his lover to appear. He could feel the heat and rhythm of the hunt now. Since leaving Chicago, Evan had missed the cosmic rush of enzymes from selecting and planning of one more offering to the Dark Lord.

When Penis Head and his man walked out, patrons turned their heads at the disgusting sight. Before Wade got in the car on the passenger's side his man embraced him, obviously sending six inches of tongue down Wade's throat, as a display of either his affection or need to revile the on-lookers. As Wade began to rub the front of his lovers pants, Evan could have killed them both right then and become a local hero.

The two men were laughing when they separated and looked around at the faces of country folk who had never seen such revulsive acts in their little town. Little did the sleepy farm community realize that the area was not just desecrated by Penis Head and his pal, but that it had become haven for the most feared serial killer ever recorded? Had the denizens known who was in the midst, they would have shuttered their doors and windows.

As the vehicle carrying Penis Head and his man left the parking lot, Wade's head disappeared below the seat. Evan could only imagine that Wade was doing bent over the driver's lap.

At last, the vehicle pulled into the parking lot of what could only be a bar. Evan drove past the small block building and looked closely at the sign out front. "The Wild Hare," with a sensual rabbit in a leather vest, top hat and tight leather pants, is home to an obviously identifiable clientele.

Evan parked across the street and after a few minutes of idling in the lot, Wade's head finally reappeared. As Wade and his lover exited the vehicle the older gent with Wade was zipping his fly and smiling. Hand in hand, the two men walked in the front door of the Wild Hare.

So, this is where people like you worship dicks and black leather." Evan said to the windshield as he watched the revolting display. "You and I will be seeing each other again, faggot. Soon, you will be with my Master.

Evan returned to the only store he knew, Fleet and Farm, where he began his detailed shopping for tools once again. This time, store security was convinced he was there to steal valuable equipment or was a cop and watched him closely.

Evan selected a tool bag first, one sturdy enough to carry a variety of tools from saws, to knives and even a battery powered Skill saw. It also had to be black, with a secure closure for concealment and washable.

From experience, Evan knew the items he wanted to supplement the items he had brought with him from Chicago, in a cardboard box. The Skill saw, for example, ran for hours on a single charge. Or so the literature insisted. With the four inch blade, Evan could saw through bone with ease and clean up would be a simple rinse with a little thinner, so as not to rust the blade.

When his selections were finalized, where he had displayed very unusual techniques for using the tools on the store's security videos, Evan headed for the check out.

"Excuse me, sir, do you come her often?" the voice said from behind him.

Evan turned to see a young man, barely old enough to shave, Evan thought. "No, actually. Why?"

"I'm an employee here, sir and I've been watching you for about one-third of my shift. Are you a cop?" the kid asked.

"Shhh, are you stupid or what, kid? Why would you asked me that, in the middle of the store where people are watching, including whoever it is that I'm here to watch. Are you that stupid? Do I need to talk to your boss or the store manager?" Evan said as he toyed with the kid he could easily kill and gut like a dear if his Master so wished.

"No, no sir. I knew you were a cop. So who're you with? The County? The State maybe?"

"Reach for the alphabet soup, kid. Reach for the soup," Evan answered.

"Holy crap. You mean like FBI?" he answered, the astonished look in his eyes.

"You're good kid. I've been doing this for years and have never been spotted and you do it in a hour or so. You're good. Maybe the Bureau can use you?

"Me? In the FBI? My mom would be proud of me. How do I get in there?"

"Well, you apply just like any other job. Then someone like me will visit you and verify what you say on the application." Evan was enjoying himself with this kid.

"Damn! Me in the FBI. Cool. Can I help you here today? Can I see your badge?"

"Keep it down, kid. I'm following a killer and you are going to get out of here before you blow my cover. You understand?"

"Ah, yes sir. Want me outside in case you need any help? I'm fast sir. Not one kid has ever outrun me here. I've caught them all," the kid boasted.

"No, my partner and I aren't arresting him here. It's too public. Don't want people hurt. Know what I mean?" Evan replied.

"You have a partner here? Where is he?"

"She, young man. She. And she is not far away from us. Her name is Rachael. Tough girl, too." Evan said.

"Damn. I didn't think of that. A girl in the FBI? I suppose they have their uses, huh?" the kid replied.

"They sure do." Evan said with a smile.

"Yeah, those long nights on stake-outs could get real interesting, huh?" the kid answered.

"More than a few times," Evan fired back with an even wider grin now.

"I got you," the kid said. "I'll be outside in the parking lot, just in case. OK?" he asked Evan.

"Sure, but if anything goes down, let us handle it. I don't want any civilians hurt here. Understood?"

"Yes sir. Are you really buying all that stuff you have in the cart?"

"Sure, the taxpayers will give it back or I'll return it later for a refund."

"I'll tell the cashier to act like you're paying for this stuff and let you leave. You can return it to me later. I guess I can trust the FBI, right?" the kid said.

"Would you like an official receipt?" Evan asked.

"Nah, that won't be necessary. Just leave it for Jason later and they'll let me know when I get back tonight. I'm here tonight too."

"Well,... thanks Jason. I'm Quentin and you'll be hearing about all this on the news, I assure you."

"Thanks. Will you be back here soon?" the kid enquired.

"I'll probably move on when the killer is done with his evil doings. I do special assignments for my boss. Life sure is a living hell like this," Evan quipped.

"See you outside, man. I mean Quentin," the kid said before walking directly towards the cashier to tell her his big plan.

"Moron," Evan said, watching him walk away.

Evan added a few more items in his cart, since he wasn't paying for them anyhow. He had always wanted a "Leatherman," with all those stainless blades, scissors and screwdrivers folded inside.

As Evan approached the cashier, she arched her back and straightened her hair. "Jason said you'd be coming here. So, you're with the FBI? That must be exciting. Does the FBI accept women? Would I have to go to school like the girl did in Silence of the Lambs'? Would I get to carry a gun?"

"Shh, can I get outta here now. I have to be in parking lot when the subject comes out of here." Evan said in a serious tone.

"Oh, of course. I'm sorry. Let me put these in a bag for you. Make it look good," she said as she placed almost five hundred dollars in items he selected into Fleet-Farm plastic bags for easy carrying.

"Thank you. And please, keep my identity a secret," Evan said in almost a whisper.

"Yes sir. Not a word from me about you being an FBI agent."

"Um, great. Have a great day. Tell Jason thanks, will you?"

"Sure. Anything to help out," she replied.

As Evan loaded his packages in the rear of the Jeep, he saw Jason, seated on a picnic table that held flowers for sale. With a two –finger salute with his right hand to his right eyebrow, which he had seen in naval movies someplace, he drove off.

"This is going to be so easy. My Master is going to be pleased," Evan said to the inside of the new vehicle.

Saving hundreds of dollars at Fleet-Farm, Evan decided to treat himself to an Italian feast at an Olive Garden that he had spotted along the road back to the motel. Sated with a mountain of cheesy lasagna, tossed salad, enough breadsticks for an angry mob and strawberry iced tea, he returned to the motel for some rest.

After trimming his fingernails and brushing his teeth, it was time for some well-deserved sleep. He needed rest, as he had a big day for his Master. Pain free, Evan fell into a deep sleep, where Penis Head Wade was suspended in the hanger.

Chapter 6

Evan Felder, the family man, worked for an insurance company in the "risk management" department, at their corporate offices downtown Chicago. As the stereotypical business computer, Evan rode the train each morning and night from the quaint suburb of Wheaton.

The city where the Felder family maintains a modest home, is slightly upscale. Not a posh community, it does, however, pride itself on cleanliness, no street gangs and a low crime rate. The city of Wheaton resembles Mayberry RFD, that a place for Chicago executives to live and raise their families in a safer environment.

When Evan began having migraine headaches, which he self-medicated with various OTC meds, he wrote them off as fatigue and stress from his job. For over a year, Evan endured and continued each day as if nothing mattered. After all, he had a family to support. He was a typical husband and father.

His co-workers finally cajoled him into setting up an appointment with a physician who routinely did work for Evan's employer and enjoyed the referrals, not to mention the income. With the preliminary tests completed, Evan continued his complaint of chronic headaches. Advising the physician that the headaches were so severe at times that he felt as if he would drop to his knees and cry out, the physicians ordered the more comprehensive tests including CT scan and MRI imagery. That is when Evan received the most detrimental news a physician can give to any patient.

Death is an inevitable as life itself. It is a cycle that has endured the Bible. A physician routinely faces the chill of death almost every day and one would believe that their constant brush with "The

Reaper" would make it far easier to break the news to a patient that their days on earth are numbered.

Evan is not old and frail, but of middle age and the American life expectancy rate of eighty-plus years, should maintain him. However, when Evan received the call from the physician to stop in his office that afternoon, Evan's heart became heavy and leaden.

The first impulse Evan had when the news of him having an inoperable tumor, so centrally buried in the core of his brain that surgery alone would kill him, he thought about suicide. The physician advised him that the pain would worsen and as the tumor grew, forcing his brain against the walls of his kill, the pain would be nothing short of excruciating. With the pain would come all the physiological side effects including loss of sleep, loss of appetite, along with the psychological effects? Once can only imagine the ancillary effects of such intense, chronic suffering from the internal combat rages on between the tumor and the brain. After all, there is only so much cranial space and when competing elements wage a war for space, the aftermath can only be described as gruesome or possibly grotesque.

Impulse aside, however, the first thought Evan had was for his family. Without him, how would they live and survive. Without him, his kids would be fatherless and the rock, upon which the fundamentals of life and mortality, would be absent.

After intense conversations with neurosurgeons, Evan was given a fairly clear picture of what lay on the horizon for him and he did not want his family to see him deteriorate and suffer. That is when he devised a plan to run off like some teen and hide until it was his time to meet death.

Evan located a "flop house," where the rates were low and the bed bugs rate was high. It was in the run down hulk of real estate, where Evan planned to spend his remaining days, literally, and save his family from the torment of watching him become more animal then human.

While on his way to a diner, where the food is free and you only pay for the grease, Evan encountered a young man called Smiley. An openly gay or should be more accurately called notoriously gay Smiley flaunted his sexuality. French kissing another man in broad daylight on a busy street was not a test of Constitutional waters, but a middle finger to all that witnessed the act.

When Evan first encountered Smiley, he was instantly sickened and the essence of being a man was challenged. The verbal tainting from Smiley only poured gasoline on the fire raging inside him and he almost skewered Smiley with an aberrant hunk of steel which lay curbside. That is, until the melee was interrupted by some smartass, who claimed to be accompanied by the Vice President or some such, which meant trouble for Evan if he persisted in his quest for street side justice.

Evan was clueless, that the man who convinced him to toss the steel back on the ground and let the two lovebirds have their fun, was an FBI agent by the name of Gibson, Melvin Gibson, hence the nickname "Hollywood," although the genesis for that moniker could easily be ordained from several of the traumatic and sometimes costly arrests Gibson had effected in various parts of the country. His last assignment, in the tropical climes of Miami, heralded the Bureau a multi-million dollar damage claim from an irate homeowner, along with a federal tort claim from the quarterback of the New England Patriots, whose powerboat Gibson commandeered for a high speed boat chase, that culminated in boats being buried in the kitchen area of a very exquisite and costly home. The net result of the naval hijinks by Gibson, earned him and his faithful partner, reassignment to the filthy streets of Chicago.

When the flood waters finally demolished the psychological dam in Evan's head, Smiley was his first "offering" to the Master that controlled the pain in his head. The voice inside his head told him what needed to be done, or the pain would become insurmountable, threatening to crack his skull. As Smiley went about his disgusting life, Evan "harvested" him for the Dark Lord.

When authorities discovered the remnants of Smiley, all that remained were the bleach-white bones, with a face stitched back in place and a driver's license to help identify him for his next of kin.

The shocking discovery, which, incidentally was in front of a major tourist attraction near the lakefront, a museum, sent chilling reports through the medial types as they sold their agencies to consumers. Once media person reported that Smiley's remains looked as though a Praying Mantis had gotten hold of him, the media instantly picked up on the lead and began referring to the psychopathic killer as "the Mantis," which stoked the fires of publicity and international fame, even more.

The Mantis infected Evan's psyche' and he became invincible, an entity that dominated mortals, all in the name and with the blessing of the Dark Lord himself. As Evan had morphed, he began to identify the voice inside his head, as that of the Dark Lord and through his benevolence, the pain would subside and Evan was afforded a somewhat carefree life, which was not bad for a man walking the Green Mile or death row, as if condemned to death by God, yet spared by Satan.

As long as Evan obeyed his Master, he was given a reprieve from pain. There was no pardon for his crimes against humanity, but a temporary stay of self-destruction was all that Evan would hope for.

Subsequently, Evan came to another brutal discovery in his fragile entomology. When a teenager, he was brutally sodomized by a bully named Quentin, who enlisted in the Army to escape the clutches of his evil father. The night before he departed for his basic training, Quentin went to a local bar, where the owner, an old "salt" from the Navy life, permitted him to sail the tumultuous seas of alcohol. When Quentin stumbled out of the bar, Evan was waiting. Clubbing Quentin over the head with a wooden bat, energized Evan gave him the satisfaction that the boy, who defiled him and made him his bitch, would never have those bragging rights again. Burying Quentin in a shallow grave, using his hands as his sole digging device, he had somehow gotten away with murder. Of course, it helped that the whole town hated Quentin and no one cared if he just disappeared, but to Evan Quentin's demise brought closure to the most embarrassing moment of his life and the chance to forget the event that haunted him since that day in the "Boys" shower in the locker room.

As time and frequency passed, Evan recognized the voice inside his head. Quentin! The boy, who has owned his soul since ramming his stiff cock in Evan's anus years ago, now controlled his life and how he lived or died.

For Evan, the game was simple. Follow the rules and obey like any soldier and he would live, pain free. To do otherwise, meant pain that would scare the sensibilities of the most fervent masochists. From the shallow grave, that has since been transformed into a gorgeous flower, Quentin managed to obtain his revenge.

The Mantis was born from the gates of Hell and brought with him, the power of the Dark Lord.

Behold.

Chapter 7

Returning to the abandoned hanger, his tool bag carrying his newly acquired items, thanks, to Jason at Fleet-Farm Security, Evan quickly changed the locking handle on the access door. The "Leatherman" folding tool carried the #2 Phillips screwdriver he used to tighten the two screws from the inside.

"There. That should do it," Evan said to the door.

The overhead door was unusable until one gained access to the locking lugs on either side, inside the hangar. Once inside, having disengaged the lugs, the push of a button marked "open," rewarded Evan with the grinding and whirring of the rotating screw which opened and closed the bi-fold door which would normally permit an airplane to be parked.

Next, Evan checked the mechanical chain hoist that was suspended from a chain, attached to the steel beam overhead. He surmised that this hangar once served as the repair station for engines, as the chain hoist would facilitate the removal and re-hanging of engines, which also explained the oily spots on the floor and boxes of spare parts that littered the place.

"Now, to make room for me to work and we're ready again," Evan said as he began to move boxes to one side of the hangar.

Once the floor was cleared of the boxes, containing meaningless parts, Evan remarked, "Now I've got room for the Jeep and my workshop."

Brushing himself off, he headed out the door and carefully checked the lock to make certain it functioned as required. That's when he noticed his fingernails needed trimming again.

"That can wait," he said to his hands. "It's time for a hunt," he said as he turned off the light inside, closed the door, which he checked again to assure himself that it was secured and strode towards the Jeep.

The sound system in the Grand Cherokee was nothing short of awesome and the local rock stations were plentiful. Evan rocked-out to Aerosmith, The Stones and Bad Company, while he admired the country side. Cows grazing in pastures on the way to his newly anointed hunting ground, calmed him and brought him a sense of tranquility he had been denied since being diagnosed with the fatal tumor.

The strip mall across the street from the Wild Hare was ideal for Evan's needs. Besides being able to get a sandwich or soda, he had access to a public restroom. As long as he spent some money in the businesses, his presence was welcomed in the lot.

Tonight, he had a singular target. John "Penis Head" Wade would soon greet the Master of All Things Unholy." If his elderly lover accompanied him, he too would find eternal bliss in the land of the Dark Lord.

Reclining the power driver's seat, Evan settled in for a long night, but was surprised by the sudden appearance of Wade and his lover.

"Ah, you have come to meet me after all" Evan said to the dashboard. After a brief period inside the Wild Hare, the two men exited and drove off in the same car he had seen them in at the Fleet Farm Store.

"Let's see where you go now," Evan said to himself as he started the engine and motored out of the lot, several car lengths behind Wade.

For almost twenty minutes, Evan tailed the two men and when they drove into a parking lot, adjoining two eight –family apartment buildings, he realized the challenge.

Unlike the crowded streets of Chicago, where traffic is an unimportant as fallen leaves, the rural confines are more noticeable and difficult.

On the second floor, the lights went on and Evan knew where they were; now all he needed was a plan to get them out of there.

Foraging around in his new tool bag, Evan came up with a new ball-peen hammer. "Perfect," he said to the hammer, as he turned it slowly in his hand, admiring the cold steel, mixed with varnished hardwood that served as its handle. "Absolutely perfect."

Evan entered the building by the rear door. True to the old adage of rural America not locking their doors, the rear door of the building did not even have a lock.

"Maybe you hillbillies are too drunk to have locks on your doors?" Evan said as he stepped inside. "Otherwise you'd spend half your time sleeping in pick-up trucks or in the barn with the critters," he mumbled.

Knocking on Penis Head's apartment door with his left hand, Evan gripped the hammer tightly in his right.

"Yeah, who's there? That you again Vega? I told you I'm not with you anymore. Go find another bitch to get you off," the voice whined from inside the apartment.

"Maintenance, asshole," Evan shouted.

"Bout time you dragged your ass here to fix the fucking tub," the voice said, just before the door swung inward and there stood the disgusting form of John "Penis Head" Wade, in briefs only, his belly reaching for the floor and hiding his genitals.

Evan planted the blunt end of the hammer squarely in the middle of Wade's huge forehead. As the hammer stuck, blood squirted and Wade fell directly to the floor.

"Oh, you're going to be problems to get out of here you tub of shit," Evan said to the unconscious man.

"Hey baby, come in here. I need some head," the voice said from the darkened bedroom.

"Coming," Evan replied sensuously, as he gripped the hammer and headed for the open door.

"Who was that, baby?" the voice asked.

"Oh, no one important. Just the fucking Reaper you faggot." Evan replied, as he stepped into the room.

There, spread-eagle on the bed, his manhood dancing to the beat of his heart as it fed the erection, laid Penis Head's man.

"Open your eyes, Gay Blade, I want you to see me," Evan said, as he held the hammer overhead and ready to strike.

"C'mon baby, put Daddy's prick in your mouth and make him cum."

"Hey, asshole, open your eyes." Evan shouted.

"Who the fuck..." the man began, but the swift descent of the hammer brought a welcome silence. The hammer landed exactly where Evan intended and the man's forehead split like an over-ripe melon.

"The Master is gonna love you two," Evan said as he wrapped the man in the bed sheets." Now, let's get you two outta here. We got a long night ahead of us."

Dragging Wade's lover by the bed sheet was easier than Evan had thought it would be. No longer caring about leaving a trail to follow, Evan dragged Wade by his hairy ankles, down the rear stairs, leaving a narrow blood tinged trail as he went. Dragging Penis Head into the shadows away from the building, Evan quickly returned to drag his lover downstairs to join him.

Loading the two men was not as difficult as Evan had imagined, reckoning the boost of strength and energy, to the excitement of the hunt.

Evan backed the Jeep silently into the hanger, the lights off and operating solely by moonlight. Once inside, he lowered the bi fold door and turned on the overhead light. When he opened the back doors of the Jeep, "blanket man" rolled out, moaning and rolling around.

"You gotta get me to the hospital. Quick. Wade hit me in the head with a hammer."

"Who are you?" Evan asked, as he tied the man's feet together with nylon rope.

"Well, Floyd, it's your lucky day. Or night, I should say. You and your boyfriend there." Evan said, as he fastened a short chair through the rope binding Finkle's feet and began hoisting him off the dusty floor.

"Hey, you can't do this. I used to work for the CIA, asshole. You know how much trouble I can cause you?"

"Spare me fag. The only trouble you're causing is in your boyfriend's ass." Evan replied and hoisted Finkle off the floor. "Now, your lover."

While dangling upside down in his underwear, Finkle watched Evan dump Wade on the floor and drag him to where he had lain moments before.

"I think your girlfriend here isn't doing so good. He's bleeding from his nose and ears. I might' a hit him too hard with the hammer."

"Let me go and I promise I won't say a word. Keep Wade. He likes little boys. What ya say?" Finkle pleaded.

Without a single word, Evan made two rapid cuts, slashing Wade from the pubis to sternum and then across his throat. Wade made no reactive movements and simply began gurgling blood through the nearly severed windpipe.

"Please, I have millions stashed in other people's names. I'll pay you. C'mon man, let me go and I'll pay you whatever you want" Finkle said, as he was hoisted higher, as Wade dangled beneath him.

Together, Wade and Finkle looked like gay ornaments on a Christmas tree, and Evan giggled.

"Would you like 'Baby' here to fellate you tonight, gay blade?" Evan asked Finkle.

"Look, I haven't seen a thing here. Just let me go and my friends at the CIA will never hear about you or this place. No one needs to get hurt here," Finkle said, as if whatever he said mattered one whit."

"Do, you ever quit acting like a bitch? Can you die like a man Floyd?" Evan asked his hands on his hips and looking up.

"Please, I have grand kids. I teach baseball to kids. I'm married, too."

"Some woman marries you and you spend your nights with this tub of shit bleeding out here and having him suck your dick? You're worse than I thought. Well, Mr. CIA, you're going to get to watch me gut your lover here like a deer. If I hear one sound out of you, "I'll stuff your cock in your mouth and tape it. You got that, Floyd? Maybe, I'll show mercy on you, if you're good."

Evan collected his tool bag from the Jeep, opened it and began laying out his tools. He could hear Floyd crying like a baby and decided to let him cry.

When Evan began on Wade, most of his intestines were already hanging out and reaching the floor. With surgical precision, Evan opened Wage with two lateral slashes, making two flaps of Wade's thorax and more organs spilled out. Removing his shirt Evan began slicing and chunks of Wage's innards splattered on the floor. Finkle's sobbing was like music to Evan and as more pieces of Wade fell off of him and landed on the floor, Finkles's crying got louder and louder.

As Evan stepped back from Wade's disemboweled body, Finkle saw Evan's arms, drenched in blood and little chunks of Wade clung to them like hamburger meat.

"I think I just saved your marriage, Floyd." Evan said.

"What?"

"Yep, I think Wade was pregnant and it looked just like you," Evan said and began laughing.

Finkle evacuated his bladder now, terror gripping him, and urine dripped from his chin to the hanger's floor.

Evan knew that he lacked the necessities to make Wade and Finkle as "sanctified" as his prior offerings, but he had an idea.

Evan lowered Wade to the concrete and untied his feet from the chain. Finkle knew that he was next and was unsure how to plead for his life.

"What's your name?" Finkle asked

"Quentin. Why?" Evan said as he stood before him.

"Quentin. Nice name. Manly. Listen, Quentin, you can't make much money doing this. How about I give you enough to retire on for life? I stole it from the government. It's yours. Just let me go. Please." Finkle said while dangling upside down.

"You're going to give me money you stole? From my government? I joined the Army to fight for my country and people like you," Evan said.

"Please don't hurt me" Finkle moaned.

"Oh, you won't feel much, you thieving faggot. As a loyal taxpayer. I appreciate your honesty now." Evan replied and picked up his fillet knife he had just finished using on Wade.

"Please," Floyd begged and raised his arms in a defensive gesture.

Evan sliced the leopard colored briefs that covered Finkle's privates. "Let's see what we have here," Evan said.

"Please, Quentin, don't hurt me."

As if slicing a Christmas ham, with steady back and forth sawing, Evan severed Finkle's cock and balls.

"This is pretty small, Floyd. I've castrated men much larger than this." Evan said as he held the bloody mess so Floyd could see it.

"Ahhggg," Floyd yelled in agony, as if he could summon some god by screaming."

While Evan held Finkle's manhood his left hand, he slashed Floyd's throat with his right. "I told you, no noise," Evan explained.

The slash was vicious, almost severing the right side of Finkle's neck. Struggling now, his hands wrapped around his wounded throat, Finkle flailed and thrashed like a shark out of water. The chain hoist rattled in protest, as it held him suspended above the ground. "Arrggh," Floyd managed to get out through the bubbles of blood.

Evan walked a few feet away, so he could watch the show and not get blood on his Fleet –Farm jeans.

"You're dying well, Floyd. Very manly," Evan commented now.

The writhing slowed to a crawl and Evan stepped forward. "Floyd can you see my Master? Is he waiting for you? See him, Floyd?" Evan asked in earnest.

When there was no response, Evan opened Floyd like he had done to Wade and began clearing out his abdomen.

It was getting late and he had work to do, before he could return to the motel and rest.

The Dark Lord was guiding him and his thoughts now. Quentin was in control.

Chapter 8

The Milwaukee offices of the FBI are located in two buildings. The primary office is within the federal building on East Wisconsin Avenue, while the "working" offices are a few blocks away.

Special Agents Mark Lanzalotti and Paul Korenoski have been partners for three years. Each had come from different cities and varied in experience. Both, however, were in their early forties and have years of service with the Bureau ahead of them.

Lanzalotti, who goes by Lanz. for short, worked in Washington, D.C. Headquarters, where he was the liaison for law enforcement agencies seeking help from the Bureau regarding potential serial killers.

Korenoski was an MP in the Army, where he became a CIS investigator, before joining the FBI. As a Criminal Investigations Division Investigator, he had handled murders on military bases, along with the investigators involving American soldiers performing atrocities on foreign nationals. His last duty station was Guatantonomo Bay, Cuba, where he arrested several soldiers for "waterboarding" detainees. When those he had arrested were released by Command officers, he decided he would not re-enlist and sought a job with the FBI.

Together, Lanz and Korenowski had aided in the capture of several murderers, who had an interstate thirst for killing.

When the call came to them from the Chicago Office of the FBI, neither was surprised.

"What makes you think this Mantis character is in our jurisdiction now, Sergeant?" Lanzalotti asked while on a conference line which included his partner, Rachael, Gibson and Perzigian.

Rachael gave some of the same synopsis she had given to Gibson and Khoren, when they came to C.P.D. headquarters last time.

"So, basically, Sergeant Hart, is you're operating off a hunch," Korenoski asked.

"No, a hunch is nothing more than a guess. This is deductive reasoning, based on what we know about this guy and the BAU profile your partner sent us from Quantico."

"Nice touch, Sergeant," Lanz said, then continued, "I like the part of our BAU people to give more credence."

Before Rachael could reply, Gibson interceded. "We operate on intuition all the time. Whether you guys call them guesses or tea leaf readings, we believe her."

"Relax people, we're not saying we don't agree that he could come our way, so tell us what we've got to work with," Lanz replied.

"Our forensics people are working to ID this guy. He's not in any of our data bases. We've tried them all. Nothing. Our guy has no arrest record whatsoever. For some damn reason, he just began killing people like lab mice." Rachael replied.

"Gibson, how's the Chicago office handling this case?" Korenoski asked.

"We're backing up the Chicago people. They've got the lead on this. Our SAC has an agreement with their Chief", Gibson answered.

"So, if he comes our way," Lanz began, "all bets are off. He's ours. No problem there?"

"Yes, actually. He's killed people in Chicago, which is my jurisdiction. We'll be bringing him back here."

"Lanz" Gibson interjected, "don't mess with this one. She ain't right in the head. Dangerous too,"

"I'll come get this guy myself, Mr. Lanzalotti. Sorry to bother you," Rachael said, as she prepared to hang up on her end.

"Hold on, Miss Hart. Let me discuss this with our SAC and see what she says. OK?" Lanz answered.

"Her?" Rachael asked.

"Yes, our SAC is a her. Why?" Korenowski replied.

"Does she have a name?" Rachael enquired.

"Nannette," Lanz, said now.

"Is she a petite blond? Used to be the police chief in Milwaukee?" Rachael asked.

"Yes, that's her. And how would you know her, Sergeant?" Lanz asked her now.

"We met at a women of law enforcement' meeting here in Chicago. We had lunch together and..."

"OK, Sergeant, we get the picture. If this guy hurts anyone here in Wisconsin, we get him first. Then you can have him," Korenoski interrupted.

"We have a capital case here, which I believe will trump your trial, but we'll let the attorneys work that out." Rachael replied as if to comfort the wounded male feelings of her counterparts.

"Mark, I think you should alert all the cities around you. I'll shoot you the BAU profile on our guy and you get them up to speed. This guy has disappeared here and I agree with Rachael. I think he's there with you now." Gibson said.

"Can anyone ID this guy for us?" Lanzalotti asked.

"I can." Gibson replied.

"And how can you ID the Mantis and he's not in your custody, Mr. Hollywoood? Korenoski asked.

"I saw the sonofabitch at a ...drop off with a media guy." Gibson almost said at the press conference, but having the Mantis amongst the top law enforcement people in Chicago, while discussing the Mantis himself, would make them the brunt of the jokesters.

"So, if he gets pulled over or picked up for vagrancy, we call you and you come here. Right?" Korenowski asked.

"I can recognize the guy in a crowd. We're sending you the pictures we have of him, too. They're not the best but you can make out the features." Gibson answered.

"All-right, we'll get word to the locals and our people. If we arrest him, we'll let you know." Lanzalotti said.

"Thanks a lot," Gibson returned.

"Yes, thanks you guys. I think I'll come there to see my friend again, Nannette." Rachael said sharply.

"That's not necessary, Sergeant. We hear you." Lanzalotti said, before disconnecting the call.

Gibson had to admit that it sounded bad that he was able to identify the Mantis, but didn't have him in cuffs.

"When I get my hands on you Mr. Mantis, I'm taking you straight to hell with me. You'll be sitting at the gates of Satan's place, you prick." Gibson mumbled.

Chapter 9

With Penis Head and Finkle, dangling from the hoist in the hanger. Evan dumped the trash bags that contained their entrails along a remote road to nowhere, headed back to the motel and took a hot shower. The water swirling around his feet was pink from the blood that coated him after a night's work of human creation and sanctification. He was quite pleased with his newest artistic touch.

After placing his clothes in trash bags and dropping them in the dumpster, Evan headed next door to the motel, to the "Cheese Castle," where he bought a sampler of Wisconsin Cheeses.

While eating a cube of sharp cheddar from a dairy whose mascot is a laughing cow, Evan began to plan his escalation to the next level. First, he needed some rest. It was morning now, after a long night of sculpting his newest works of art and would make ready for the grand finale.

But, Evan could not sleep, so he ate his cheese and made instant coffee in his room. The voice in his head was strong and resonant. He was pain free and felt fine. He showered again, this time in cold water, shaved, brushed his teeth with a penchant to curtail the yellowish patina and trimmed his nails again. He was ready to become a national figure. He had to stop at a hardware store and Fleet –Farm was no longer safe for him. Farm communities live on hardware and finding one was only a matter of driving a couple more blocks.

With everything he needed and the seats of the Jeep folded down, Evan still had room for Wade and Finkle.

"There you go, you two love birds. I am giving you immortality tonight. You should thank me, and you are with my Master, so I envy you. I'll join you soon enough, but tonight you make history,"

Evan said in all sincerity after hoisting them into the back of the Jeep.

The Wild Hare was busy, as cars surrounded the building. Some sort of musical noise poured out onto humanity, as Evan went about his chores. A couple times, men waved to him as they entered the club. One held his crotch and licked his lips, while eyeing Evan over. He had a T-shirt that said "It Ain't Gonna Lick Itself," with a pink tongue. Evan just smiled and continued working.

When Evan had finished, he retrieved the cordless drill from the Jeep and using the Phillips driver, sunk three, four-inch wood screws into the front and rear doors. The screws were long enough to prevent the opening or closing of either door. To Evan's delight, not one patron attempted to leave or enter, which made his tasks much simpler.

Wade and Finkle were laid out under the sign with the naughty rabbit in leather pants. It was time!

Evan opened the hood of the Jeep and attached the black "ground" wire of the jumper cables, while he held the red clamp inches above.

"Say hello to my Master, you sick bastards," Evan said and brought the red clamp to the positive terminal on the SUV's battery.

In rapid succession, six cans of gasoline, which Evan had placed around the building and lowering homemade "stingers," made of two pieces of metal with an insulator of some sort to prevent contact, while attached to separate wires, into the cans. The string of incendiary devices were, in electrical vernacular, wired in series and as current passed from one to the next, which caused a spark and heat inside the gas cans, the can exploded, sending the flaming liquid onto the sides of the Wild Hare.

Wade and Finkle were laid out, side-by-side, holding hands. The sign right above them with the naughty rabbit would become a nationally televised image, albeit with bloody sheets draped over the two lovers.

Leaning against the Jeep humming some incoherent melody, Evan watched the flames devour the sides of the Hare. When the roof caught fire, Evan knew that soon he would hear the frantic voices from inside the fated club.

Suddenly, the music stopped and Evan could hear shouts from inside. When some moron threw a chair out a window, Evan giggled as oxygen fed the infantile flames that licked at the ceiling inside. A whoosh of fire blew out the remaining windows and Evan could feel the heat rush past him.

When Evan heard the screams from inside the inferno, he began dancing a jig of some sort, while laughing wildly.

"Oooh, it's hot tonight, Gonna make this place look just right. When the Master arrives, he'll see I've harvested all these lives," Evan chanted..

When Evan was sure that no one had survived the blaze, he bid Wade and Finkle farewell and drove away. On the stereo inside the Jeep, he was rocking to the sound of Bruce Springsteen shouting "Born in the U.S.A." and he sang along.

"This is Sergio," the Chicago station chief said as he answered his cell phone.

"Quentin, here. You might want to get a crew to the Wild Hare in the little place called Racine, up here in Wisconsin, I just sent some faggots to meet my Master," Evan explained.

"Wait, let me pull over. You did what now?"

"I said, I just sent a bunch of ass-pirates to hell up here in Wisconsin. This is just the beginning. You got what you paid for Good-night. I'll be in touch again, soon." Evan said and hung-up, before tossing the cell phone out the window and into the cool night air. "Where to now, Evan," he said to himself. "Where to now."

While Evan showered, the local fire department was battling to save the surrounding buildings near the Wild Hare. When Evan had changed clothes and was on the road again, having loaded his tools and said his farewells to the hanger the Dark Lord gave him to work in; charred bodies were being laid out around the parking lot.

"How do we know it's our guy?" Lanzalotti asked Gibson.

"Because I received a call from our twenty-four hour line that the station chief for Associated Press here in Chicago, said the Mantis called him and told him all about it." Gibson replied.

"You going to talk to this guy?"

"I'm on my way to his home right now and Rachael is meeting me there. We intend on getting some real answers from this guy, too." Gibson exclaimed.

"I'm on my way to the Wild Hare place now. What I hear isn't good, Gibson." Lanzalotti said.

"What's he do up there?" Gibson asked.

"Well, the preliminary reports I get, say that there were nineteen men inside the building. All toasted, extra crispy. Seems our boy has a sense of pyromania in him. Asshole wrapped the building in gas cans and wire, and then started the bastard on fire. Oh, and he screwed the doors shut. Nice touch, huh?"

"He fried nineteen people?" Gibson asked.

"Well, not exactly people in my book. Pedophiles mostly, with a salty mixture of homosexuals. They've identified an attorney named by the name of Victor Vega, who we had on radar for child porn, along with a few of our most notable pee-pee touchers."

"My, your sensitivity training went well at Quantico, not to mention those politically correct classes you must have missed." Gibson mused.

"These are not my favorite people. I'm a father and I worry about assholes like these." Lanzalotti said.

"Yeah, just don't refer to them as pee-pee touchers in the 302's or you'll be stamping out campfires in Wyoming," Gibson replied, using the words of his own SAC if he screwed this case up.

"Should I include the little detail about their heads?" Lanzalotti teased.

"What about their heads?" Gibson asked.

"Both of our guys out front had their heads inside their abdomen, with their manhood proudly stuffed inside their mouths. Nice work, huh?"

"This guy cuts their heads off, hollows them out like pumpkins at Halloween and stuffs their heads inside?" Gibson asked in dismay.

"Yep! That about sums it up, except for the items stuffed in their mouths, of course. Seems our guy doesn't like penises being located where they normally are. Does that say anything?" the Milwaukee agent asked.

"Seems like he may have been a victim some time and in his own way, he is telling us. " Gibson answered.

"This is the sickest bastard I've ever seen. Hell, we had cannibals here in Wisconsin, but making people into Halloween decorations is really crazy."

"I made a promise to myself that this asshole and I were going to have a private meeting when I find him," Gibson said.

"I didn't hear that. Right now, we gotta find this asshole. My boss is all over me. The news is on me. The wife demands his capture. The kids draw pictures of the Mantis with green Crayon. And I've only had this case a couple of days." Lanzalotti explained.

"Then, you should thank me. If it weren't for us making it too hot for him here, he wouldn't be there and giving you all that media attention." Gibson taunted.

"Yeah. A great career boost, if we don't get this guy quick. I imagine your SAC isn't too pleased either."

"This isn't going to help," Gibson explained." My SAC is going to hit the roof when he hears this asshole just fried nineteen people up there. Shows Rachael was right though."

"Yeah, she had that pegged right. I hear she's quite the looker," Lanzalotti said.

"Whoa, that girl is deadly as a viper, but capable of being Miss America. Did I forget to mention that she teaches martial arts?" Gibson said, chuckling.

"Damn attractive combination, you ask me."

"Her boyfriend is one of the top ten martial artists in the world. I've seen videos of him and Bruce Lee had nothing on him. I'd be careful, if I were you."

"Point made. I still can dream, can't I? Lanzalotti joked.

"Yeah, just don't try touching. It could send you on disability income."

"Let me know what this AP guy worked out with our killer and how long they've been playing grab-ass, will you?" Lanzalotti asked.

"Shortly, I'll be at his place in about ten clicks and will call you back," Gibson replied.

"Hey, Gibson, I want you to know that you don't seem as bad as your reputation has you," the Milwaukee Special Agent stated.

After a brief pause, while Gibson tried to conjure up something, witty in response to the accolade, he said, "Thanks. I love you, too."

Through the laughter on Lanzalotti's end, Gibson heard him say, "Strike that, Gibson, you're back on asshole status" before the connection was broken.

"Sergio Medrano?" Gibson asked the man who answered the door. Without waiting for an answer, he continued. "Special Agent Gibson. FBI. We talked earlier on the phone?"

"How did you know where I live?" Sergio said before he had a chance to think about the question. "Oh, I guess...well, come in please."

"Thank you. Do you have any coffee? We're going to be awhile, Mr. Medrano. We need your complete cooperation on this. You understand?"

"Of course. Our attorney has been here since I called you earlier. We've been waiting for someone to call or show up. Please join us." Sergio said, inviting Gibson into his home in Oakbrook.

For the next three hours, which can only be described as grueling for Gibson, almost every question he asked earned him a protestation of "we've done nothing illegal" from the local attorney for the Associated Press.

When the session was over, Gibson had been assured complete cooperation and arranged for the techies downtown to tap Sergio's cell phone with a "trap and trace" device, called a "Pen register." When the Mantis called next, the number would be captured and traced, using the "cell cite location" of where the call originated from.

Cell phones, which are nothing more than fanciful walkie-talkies, need the connection to towers, which then route the calls through a network of towers and hand-lines. When a cell phone is either answered or used to place a call, the nearest tower is identified as the "cite" that facilitated the connection. This is often confused with the Global Positioning System, where satellites do all the tracking and locating. Locating cell phones is much easier.

In addition to the trap and trace, Sergio had agreed to monitoring of his calls, so that when the Mantis called again, they would have a recording and voice print as evidence.

When Gibson departed the Medrano home, he suffered a mixture of exhaustion and anticipation. As any good cop understands, lives are at risk and if Sergio Medrano was contacted by the Mantis, it meant that one or more people had just lost their lives.

Chapter 10

Evan's life at the moment was nothing short of glorious. Not only was he pain free, he had spent the morning switching from station to station, as he listened to the outrageously flattering reports of his Wild Hare incineration of nineteen men.

At first, Evan was caught off guard when the reporters discussed the blaze as an attack by some vigilante group against the pedophiles inside the hellish conflagration. Killing registered sex offenders was not Evan's problem, being a father himself and a citizen who had supported capital punishment for such human filth. What irked Evan was the original announcement that some citizen group , tired of the pedophiles flaunting themselves at the Wild Hare, was responsible for the destruction and not the Mantis.

A short time later, every channel had the news that the FBI had just announced that the murders at the Wild Hare were actually the work of the man Chicagoans had come to know as the Mantis. An interview with Special Agent Mark Lanzalotti had confirmed that the Mantis was responsible beyond any doubt and "efforts were being made to locate the subject now."

"Even if I gave you my name, you assholes, you couldn't stop me," Evan said with a sneer at the Jeep's stereo. "The Master would have you all for a picnic in his world," Evan said fighting laughter.

In reality, Evan was wishing more and more each day, that the Dark Lord would finally summon him to the land he sought for eternal life. He had been a faithful servant and soldier, after all and wanted his reward. However, his work was not yet finished.

The Jeep seemed to point itself westward and as Evan drove along, he drank in the sights of the dairy farms, fertile cropland with the monolithic machines that tilled soil planted the seed and then harvested the crops.

The Evan Felder side of him wished he had had the foresight to bring his family to Wisconsin, with its tranquil lifestyle and desire to keep it that way. Only cities like Milwaukee and Racine, with their close proximity to Chicago, was infested with street gangs, where hoodlum youths shot at each other to prove how manly they were, or how miserable a marksman.

Overall, the further Evan drove westward, the farms got more plentiful and larger in size. When he neared La Crosse, he came upon a road sign which read, "Welcome to God's Country" and he began a demonic laugh. "God has no power over the Dark Lord you assholes. You'll see when he comes to harvest all of you," Evan snarled to the Jeep's windshield, as he gripped the steering wheel.

He began to relax when he entered the "Land of a Thousand Lakes," Minnesota, leaving "God's Country" east of the state line.

Evan had no idea where he was going and was leaving that decision to fate. When he stopped for lunch, local news even reported the brutal killings by the Mantis, who now had a fan club according to the personnel at Facebook, along with a logo, which consisted of a pair of eye's staring directly at you.

"Can I help you, sir?" the plump waitress asked.

"I hope that Mantis character isn't around here. He sounds pretty scary" Evan said, repressing a smile.

"Nah, he doesn't want any part of Minnesota. We ain't got many pedophiles here. We give them people life in prison, so our kids are safe, unlike most states that give them probation or slap on the hand. Can I take your order?" she finally asked.

Without reason whatsoever, Evan felt starved and ordered two cheeseburgers, fries, onion rings and a Diet Coke. When the food arrived, the table looked as if two people were eating lunch, as Evan had neatly divided the items and was eating only one of the cheeseburgers and the onion rings, while the other burger with French Fries was cooling across from him.

When Evan had refueled the Jeep, he bought a baseball cap with a patch seven on with a large, colored fish, seemingly taking a fishing lure in his gaping mouth.

"Would you like me to cut the tag off the hat for you?", the clerk asked.

"Sure. Anything interesting going on around here?" Evan asked, wondering if the Milwaukee news had reached this far.

"Oh my, the priests still want to get married and cause a ruckus," she said, snipping the plastic tie that held the price tag to the cap.

"What priests?" Evan asked.

"It's all over the news. Look, she said, pointing to the rack of newspapers.

Facing Evan were several newspapers each with its own photo of two men, some in priestly attire and some in regular clothes. "Gay Priests Demand Church Wedding" one headlined. "I'll take this too," Evan said as he took one of the newspapers.

Once inside the Jeep, Evan read the story of the two excommunicated priests from San Francisco, who had received the boot, instead of the pope's blessing, after formally seeking the Catholic Church to permit them to be married under California law.

"Excuse me father for I have sinned," Evan said to the newspaper. "Or, is it 'pardon me'?" Evan argued to himself. "No, that would be if someone makes a mistake. The mistake you two made, was gaining the attention of my Master, who is far more powerful than the son of a slave you worship."

The news article reported that the defrocked priests now reside in Edina, a suburb of Minneapolis and not that distant from where he was then. Out of knowing, more than planning, the Jeep headed towards the "Twin Cities" and meeting the priests.

Once in Edina, it was simple to locate the parish that afforded the two priests a temporary shelter, till they make more permanent arrangements. The towns-people were more than happy to give another tourist a guiding hand.

Arriving at the quaint church at suppertime, he noticed the adjoining structure had smoke rising from behind, indicating an outdoor grill most likely.

Parking the Jeep almost a block away, Evan reached for his tool bag and located his fillet knife, sliding it up his left sleeve.

Walking back towards the church, Evan felt the power of the Dark Lord surge through his moral body and becoming his armor, as he was about to enter the house of his nemesis and carry out his Master's will.

As he walked around the rear of the apartment sized structure that was attached to the Church of Christ, he saw a young man turning hot dogs on a grill, with metal tongs.

"Smells good" was all Evan could think of to gain the cook's attention.

Turning to face, him, Evan recognized the man as one of the two gay priests.

"Would you like one? We have plenty," the man now known as Paul Shurack, not Father Shurack, asked.

"I don't want to interrupt your cookout. I just came by to see if there are any weeknight services being held here," Evan said in return.

"You're not from here, are you?"

"It's that apparent? No, Father, I'm from Chicago and just visiting friends up here."

"Well, sit down and break bread with us then. It's good to have a friendly face here." Shurack said.

Evan noted that Shurack didn't correct him when he referred to him as "Father," which told him that he missed his role in the Church. "Well, I have been on the road a while. OK."

"Good. Robert, I mean, Father Hade, will be here shortly. He's doing a radio interview in the cities and should be back pretty quickly."

"You sure you have enough? I don't want to impose." Evan said while looking around for any tell-tale signs of anyone else being present.

"No, it's just him and I. You don't need to fret about that. We have more than enough." Shurack responded.

"Is there someplace I can wash my hands before we eat?"

"Sure, the kitchen's right inside the patio door. Don't mind the boxes. We're being reassigned to another parish and are getting ready to move on. We're really looking forward to the challenge of a new parish too." Shurack said, still pretending to be a "Man of the Cloth."

The rogue priest was accurate about one thing, as the kitchen was strewn with cardboard boxes. Evan ran the water in the sink as he quickly looked in the adjoining rooms for other people. Seeing no one he returned to the kitchen and turned the water off. Handling one of them at a time was more than he had hoped for. The Master was looking out for him, in the den of liars serving a false prophet.

Returning to the back yard, Evan approached the ex-priest and silently withdrew the fillet knife from his sleeve.

"Find everything all...," Shurack said as he turned towards Evan, a hot dog resting between the tines of a metal tongs.

Evan plunged the wicked blade into Shurack's abdomen and sawed his way upward until he felt the bone of Shurack's sternum.

Being face-to-face, mere inches from a man as you take his life, is an experience that combat veterans spend a life time trying to repress. For Evan, watching Shurack's expression and absolute helplessness at the method by which he was being murdered, was intoxicating for 'Evan. It was if some unseen black lightening flashed across his eyes and a fire burned in his eye sockets. The dying priest could not take his eyes off Evan's and knew that his soul was on the fast track to Hell.

Shurack knelt before Evan, blood streaming from his mouth and abdomen, as the wounded heart and cardiac arteries continued to pump blood as if all was unharmed. His hands clutched Evan's trousers on the sides and his head was up turned, as if he wanted to ask Evan why he had done this.

With fire in his eyes, the spirit of the Dark Lord coursing through his veins and arteries, Evan was unwilling to show the ex-priest that his god may save him from the Master's maw. With a kick of his foot, the dying man lay on the grass, clutching his open thorax in a useless attempt to starve off death. The hot dog he had offered Evan lay on the ground in front of the ex –priest's contorted face.

While the dying man watched, Evan reached down and picked up the scorched hot dog and began eating it with a bloody hand. "Don't mind if I do. Thank you. We don't want this to go to waste now, do we"

When Shurack's eyes no longer saw and his mind no longer thought. Evan began his Master's work. Just as he knelt over the dead man, he heard a voice from inside the building.

"Paul, you here?" the voice said.

"Help. Help Me." Evan shouted.

A young man sprinted from the building and to Evan's side. "My God, what happened here," the defrocked priest said in anguish, as he quickly examined his "life partner."

"I heard a scream and came running" Evan said, as he held the fillet knife behind his back.

"Paul," the man shouted, as if he could call him back from Hell.

Not wanting the dead man's lover to piece together what must have occurred, he got closer to Hade, the second defrocked priest from the newspaper. As Hade cradled Shurack in his arms and weeping a lover's tears of sorrow, Evan jammed the blade directly into the back of Hade's neck. The thrust was so forceful, the experienced blade snapped, leaving Evan only the wooden handle to defend himself with, if Hade's god somehow willed him to survive.

But Hade's god had no such empathy for the ex-priest and Hade began to thrash around on the grass. The blade's tip was protruding from the front of Hade's neck. As he struggled to try to remove the offensive steel from his throat, he slashed his fingers on the sharp blade. Surprisingly, the amount of blood loss was minor, in comparison to that of Shurack.

Through the gurgling sound emitted from the severed larynx, Hade was trying to pray now.

"Your Lord can't help you, gay blade. My Master sent me here to bring you to him. Can you see Him, priest? Can you see the land of my Master? "Evan asked, as he knelt next to Hade.

The last vision Hade ever saw was the fire red eyes of what could only be Satan himself as he knew that he was doomed to an eternity in perdition for his sins against God and the church.

Quickly, Evan dragged the dead men to the center of the yard. Retrieving a clever and butcher knife from the kitchen, he began his Master's work.

Chapter11

"You're not going to believe what this fucking maniac did," Lanzalotti said. "Oops, sorry Rachael, I forgot you were on the line."

"I've heard worse around here, but thanks for the chivalry," she replied.

"Anyhow, our Mantis freak now turns up in Edina, Minnesota last night. Visited two priests, or ex-priests I should say, who came there from San Francisco, the homosexual capital of the world. Seems these two guys met there and fell helplessly in love and asked the Catholic Church to marry them."

"There's a new twist," Gibson said on the speaker phone on the desk in the conference room inside the FBI offices in Chicago, where he was joined by his partner and Rachael.

"Yeah. The Associated Press did a small article on it a few months back. Said the Pope went bananas about these two and kicked them to the curb, the Milwaukee agent said.

"I never heard anything about it, but then again, I'm Irish," Rachael replied.

"You haven't heard the whole thing yet. I get the call at home last night from an agent in our office in Minneapolis. He got the call because of the alert we put out about this guy's MO." Langzalotti said.

"What MO?" Gibson asked.

"He cut their heads off and placed them on their open abdomens, while he laid them out in an upside down cruciform position behind the Church of Christ. Then, we presume it was our guy, pilled a barbeque grill inside a kitchen area in an adjacent building where the Church permitted these guys to stay until more permanent housing was found and damn near burnt the whole church to the ground. Pretty extensive damage to the place, too, as I understand it."

"This guy has really lost it," Rachael commented.

"Lanz, are you issuing a statement confirming that this was the work of our boy?" Gibson asked.

"The Minneapolis SAC is discussing that with Washington right now. Otherwise, the gay rights people will scream that we're not doing our jobs, because they like male parts, not women." Lanzalotti explained.

"We don't want wannabe warriors try to take credit for cleaning up the streets and making the heterosexual lifestyle the norm again," Khoren pointed out.

"Yeah, we're getting crack-pot calls already, each trying to take credit for the murders. We'll track them down in due time and arrest them for the calls, but right now our focus is on finding the lunatic."

"Any idea where he's going next?" Gibson asked.

"That's why I'm calling you people. Rachael seems to have some connection with this guy and knows where to look next. Plus, your Associated Press guy should have gotten a call by now."

"Mr. Lanzalotti," Rachael began, "it has just occurred to me that you're an asshole. Perhaps we can train together one of these days?"

"No thanks. I'm not into fighting women," he answered.

"Before you two get carried away, stop right there. I'm sure Lanz didn't mean it like that." Gibson said fatherly.

"Nothing has come into Medrano's phone yet, but I'll alert our tech guys to be prepared for the call. We want a quick cell cite location, so we can saturate the area with people," Khoren interjected.

"Khoren, the minute that site is located, call me and our office in Minneapolis. We need to know if this guy is headed back to us here in Wisconsin. "Lanzalotti said.

"We need to stop chasing this guy" Rachael said.

"What? We should just let his guy run loose?" the Milwaukee agent shouted into the phone.

"That's not what I said, Mr. FBI" Rachael returned sarcastically. "I said we should stop chasing him, not arresting him."

"What do you mean, Rachael" Khoren said softly.

"Like McArthur did to the Desert Fox, Rommel. We want this guy to come to us. We can't chase this guy all over the goddamn country. We don't even know who he is," she replied. Then, after taking a deep breath, continued. "Listen, we need to draw him to us, where we can take him down."

The idea caught everyone off guard and the silence confirmed federal minds at work.

"And how would you do this, Rachael," Khoren asked.

"We have our own Wild Hare. A place where the Mantis can hate and feel drawn to by whatever evil forces that guide him," she replied.

"Let me get this straight." Lanzalotti began, "we ask the federal government to buy some nightclub which we then name the Wild Hare, hoping the Mantis pays us a visit?"

"Something like that," she replied now.

"She might be on to something gentlemen. I'm sure the Marshals have some nightspot we confiscated in a drug case. We use that. Change the name; let our techs wire it up for sound and video. Could work!" Khoren exclaimed in support.

Another round of silence proclaimed federal minds at work again.

"I can get our AP guy to get word out to the media that Chicago's Wild Hare is as nefarious as the one he destroyed there in Wisconsin," Gibson said now.

"Are we buying into this idea everyone?" Lanz asked.

"It makes sense. She's right. We can't continue to chase a phantom," Khoren explained. "I'm on board."

"Beats sitting around waiting for the next news flash to come in, where this guy toasted someone," Gibson joined in.

"Hang on people, I'm looking at the U.S. Marshals inventory list of seized real estate and we have a possible winner," Khoren interrupted. "A few weeks ago, they got a clear title to a nightclub they seized as being from drug money. It's going to auction in six months. We can probably use it. Anybody interested?"

"All-right let's say everyone agrees to this idea. How do we get our killer here and bust him?" Lanzaolotti asked.

"We call this place the Wild Hare and get some AP coverage or local news," Rachael began then stopped and looked at Gibson. "You said our guy hasn't called the AP contact yet, right?"

"Correct," Gibson answered, then realized where she was headed.

"So, we have him tell our guy about the new Wild Hare and how they're worried about the killings in Wisconsin happening to their club. He can tell him that the AP has even sent a crew there to interview the owner and see if he's concerned." Rachael said.

"I draft the scenario for my partner to give the guy when he calls," Khoren said bluntly.

"How do we get the building?" Rachael asked.

I'll take care of that, after I get the draft done for Gibson. I'll get the building, don't worry," Khoren stated as if in command.

After a brief, pause at Khoren's jumping into the mix as he did, Rachael said,

"I'll get the building painted. I have some guys serving community service that need the work hours or go to jail again."

"I'll get the techs to wire it up so we have audio and visual, three sixty." Gibson said.

"And what would you like us to do in Milwaukee? Lanzalottti said.

"You can bring the brats," Gibson said and everyone began laughing.

"I'm going to change the script a bit," Khoren said and waited for the laughter to cease. "I'm going to have our AP guy tell this maniac that the new Wild Hare is going full throttle and they don't have room for all the customers. That it's all attributed to him burning the place in Wisconsin and the owner is becoming rich off the Mantis."

"Hmm, there's an idea. I like it Khoren. See why you're my partner?" Gibson joked.

"I'm you're partner because Captain America turned you down as stunt double. Remember, opposites attract. I'm the brains." Khoren said.

"So, I'm the muscle?" Gibson asked.

"You're the weapon of mass destruction George Bush spent years trying to locate." Khoren answered back.

"Ouch. Any other brainy things to say?" Gibson said jokingly.

"Yes, actually. We're going to tell this crazy bastard that the Catholic Church has set new attendance records all because the Mantis appears to have declared war on it." Khoren answered.

"Should we let the Church know that we're going to use it as partial bait?" Rachael asked.

"Should we let the Church know that we're going to use it as partial bait?" Rachael asked.

"Maybe the Milwaukee office can add that to the brats?" Gibson mused.

"You're an asshole, Gibson. If you were assigned to Milwaukee, we'd have you counting peckerwoods at truck stops." Lanzalotti replied.

And so it was, in a mere two days' time, the new Wild Hare stood proudly it up, murals of famous men painted on its walls. Brando, Fonda, McQueen and Eastwood, from various scenes of movies in which they starred. The inside was barren. Not a bar stool or booth. The "patrons," who stood outside and smoked, we were all cops and federal agents. The "owner" was an ATF Agent named Adamson, who fit the role to a tee, with his rogue appearance and smart mouth.

On surrounding buildings, remote cameras had been mounted, so that the surveillance team in the FBI's eighteen wheeler, which was parked a block away in an abandoned warehouse, could manipulate the cameras and watch the building from all sides and the roof.

Sergio Medrano finally received the call from Evan, who could not resist bragging about the priests he had slain and how he watched the Dark Lord claim their souls in the last grasps for life. When Medrano, who followed Khoren's draft and coaching to the letter, told Evan of the national impact he had every time his name was mentioned. Feedings Evan's unholy ego was a key component to leering him back to Chicago. In telling Evan that he was such a celebrity instead of mad-dog killer, Khoren played to Evan's need for stardom. As Perzigian and Gibson played the recording for Rachael, Calvin Gillings, Ben Ori, Lanzalotti and the Korenenoski, who had assembled to finalize the plan, all were impressed with how Khoren had tuned in to the Mantis, his needs and what would most likely bring him to them.

After Evan had promptly disposed of the disposable phone he had purchased at a truck stop outside of Minneapolis, the FBI was already in contact with the phone's service provider to obtain the cell cite location.

Evan was flattered and incensed after talking to Sergio Medrano. He was unaccustomed to being even slightly manipulated and he felt that Medrano was trying to do just that. Something was amiss, yet Evan was unable to identify what it was. He expected the FBI to record Medrano's calls, hence the disposable phones. He even accepted that the FBI would get AP station chief to cooperate in locating him. After all, Evan was no fool. Everything Medrano had told him was harmless and truthful, as Evan had witnessed the impact the Mantis had on people. Yet something was wrong or misplaced and it disconcerted Evan.

Evan could feel the magnetic pull; the absolute need to return home. He intended to see the surgeon who had diagnosed him as "terminal," where he could look at him and tell him why he was aging in appearance, his hands becoming claw like and the constant red replacing the white in his eyes. Perhaps Evan thought, the tumor has grown or about to burst?

He headed the Jeep east on I-94 and headed home.

Chapter 12

The public condemnation of the senseless murders of the two priests, even though they were excommunicated from the Catholic Church, along with the satanic positions in which they were left, rang from on high within the church administrators.

What began with a Monsignor talking to local media about the loss of life and obvious hatred for Jesus Christ and the Church, mounted exponentially? As the name or reference to the Mantis escalated in the media, the Catholic Church issued a new declaration of outrage at how media hucksters were portraying the killer as some knight or vigilante from Hell.

The newly ordained Cardinal from Chicago reached out to the Attorney General of the United States, himself a Catholic, for leads or current status in capturing the killer. Nothing.

The Cardinal then paid a personal visit to the FBI offices in Chicago, where he met privately with Calvin Gillings for over an hour. When he left, he was left with the impression that the FBI was unwilling to share information.

With reluctance, the Cardinal sent a lengthy Memo by private courier, the Vatican, detailing the events and lack of the law enforcement cooperation in the quest to identify and capture the person responsible for killing the priests and offending the church.

In Rome, papal confidantes quietly met with "Friends of Friends," which in America is notoriously referred to as the Mafia, or organized crime. The Bible may speak of vengeance being not in the hands of mortals, but the Pope, who is poised at the right hand of the Holy Spirit, is above mortality. With the blessing of the Vatican, the "friends" are asked for help in finding the man called mantis.

Daniel Salvino, the warrior seen so often in full –contact matches around the world, along with being madly in love with a Chicago cop named Rachael Hart, is also known as "Savior" in a very secretive group called the "Praetorian Guard." Savior is known to the Commissioner, which rules the five crime families in America, as their leader and chief executive when security matters arise. When he was summoned to New York, where he met with the head of the Commission on a private jet, he was given a difficult assignment.

"Daniel, we have been asked by the Vatican to help locate and capture the person or persons responsible for murdering two priests in Minnesota. We, meaning the Commission, have assured the Vatican that we will do whatever possible to help," the Commissioner said.

The jet was circling over the Atlantic Ocean, until the pilots were given the word to return to base. Daniel was looking out at the pitch black below, as he considered the implications of the Commissioner's directives.

"I have two problems with this matter," Daniel began.

"First, I do not know when and we do the Pope's bidding when it's a mortal sin in the first degree. Second, the case is too close to me and could expose me and the Guard."

"Daniel, this man who calls himself Mantis, killed two Priests."

"Correction, sir, two excommunicated gay priests who asked the Church to marry them." Daniel interrupted.

"The Pope has asked us for help. What would you like me to tell them?" the Commissioner asked.

"Was the request from the Vatican to terminate this guy or capture him?" Daniel asked.

"The request was not specific David. What are you getting at?"

"We treat it as a request to capture, and not harm this Mantis. Would that be fair?" Daniel asked.

After a moment, the Commissioner responded. "Yes, I think the Church couldn't argue about this guy facing justice. After all, it's wrong to kill people, to show that killing people is wrong. Right? Wasn't that the saying from the 60's and 70's?" The Commissioner asked with a smile.

"Yes, sir, that would reflect the sentiment of that time."

"Now, what about the second concern of yours? Is that solved now?" the Commissioner enquired.

"No, sir, it's not solved. Because this is so close to me, I cannot involve the other members of the Guard directly. So, with your approval, I will see that this Mantis is given over to the police."

"Daniel, we have been working together for a very long time. You are the foundation for our family and how you decide to handle this matter is yours to decide. Alone, you are a formidable army." The Commissioner intoned.

"Then, you may send word to the Vatican that the Praetorian Guard will handle this little matter for them. Ironic though, isn't it sir?"

"What's that Daniel?" the Commissioner said after alerting the pilots to return to home.

"The Praetorians protected Ceaser, who once put Jesus to death and now, the Praetorians are protecting the believers." Daniel replied.

"The Lord works in mysterious ways, Daniel. We are only here for his amusement, I think."

Daniel had laid some personal ground rules for this matter. He would not use Rachel as a means to get information by whatever means necessary, he would assure Rachael's safety, even if it meant exposing him to the law.

He would only need the long-distance assistance of one guardsman, who has hacked into every computer system known to mankind. Gaining illegal access to the FBI data bases was his entertainment and that would give me all he needed to know and insulate the woman he adored.

Chapter 13

"He is demanding a Black Mass" Rachael explained to Ben.

"OK, sit down and tell me about this. Who is demanding a Black Mass?"

"The Mantis. He called Medrano, our AP contact and told him that if a Black Mass isn't performed at the Cathedral he'll destroy a church." Rachael said.

"The Cardinal will never agree to that, Rachael. A Black Mass would desecrate the Cathedral. What's our next option?" Ben asked now.

"According to Mr. Medrano, who's afraid for his family now, he wants the Mass videotaped and placed on U-tube, so the world can watch."

"Medrano isn't pulling any kind of publicity crap here, is he?" Ben asked.

"We have a copy of the phone call. The FBI sent it over and already located where the call originated from. Another interesting piece of information, too."

"And?" Ben asked, slightly perturbed at having to cross –examine her in order to hear the whole story.

"He's on his way back here. The last two calls are in succession. The first in the Minneapolis area and this one from the Madison, Wisconsin areas, hear the Interstate there. He'll be back in Chicago by tonight." Rachael said flatly.

Ben leaned back in his chair and studied Rachael for a moment. "And what's your plan, Sergeant?"

"We tell him we agree." She responded.

"Oh? And how are you going to convince the Cardinal to permit his mass in the Cathedral?"

"We aren't, Ben. We're going to seal off the Cathedral as if we were filming and wait for this guy to come to us."

"And what if this guy wants proof of the mass going on inside?" Ben enquired.

"Simple enough. I already located footage of what a Black Mass looks like and can play that for him. He won't know the difference, Ben,"

"You discussed this with the feds?" he asked her with a wry smile.

"It's our case, Ben. We don't need to ask their approval for everything we do. No, I am not discussing this with the feds. "Rachael replied sternly.

"I'll talk to the Cardinal and explain the plan. He's an old poker buddy of mine. He's pretty good, too. I always said that if he failed as a priest, Las Vegas would be scared of him." Ben replied.

"I'll make the arrangements with the Traffic Division to cordon off the area and we'll get the news people to make it look authentic."

"How we going to know if he shows up, Rachael?"

"He'll need to get inside the Cathedral, like he did the press conferences. We'll give him just one way into the place and no way out."

"And the Cardinal? How are we going to protect him? In case this guy decides to work his way up the ladder to killing God last?" Ben asked her.

"I'll ask Daniel to watch him. If a cop is around him, the Mantis may smell the trap. If Daniel, who's known not to be a cop, is around the Cardinal, then he may figure Daniel is just his security. "Rachael said.

"And your boyfriend will just jump at the idea of being dragged into this?"

"I'll convince Daniel, Ben. He'll do it," she said with her cheeks blushing and an impish smile on her face.

Ben had little doubt that Daniel would do anything Rachael asked of him, as would he himself. Rachael just had that kind of power.

"I'll tell the Cardinal that he's going to have the pleasure to meet and spend a day or two with one of the world's top martial artists. He'll love that." Ben responded.

"Should I invite Gibson to the party, Ben?" Without hesitation, Ben replied. "He can ID this guy Rachael. I think you need him."

"Yeah, good point."

"He's not a bad guy, Rachael. He's one of the best fibbies I've ever seen, actually." Ben said.

"Maybe" she replied and walked out of his office. In less than fourteen hours, they would make it appear as if a Black Mass were being held at the Cathedral, at the demand of the Mantis.

What Rachael believed would be the toughest part of the operation, was convincing Daniel to protect the Cardinal. He had just returned from New York on business and was eager to train for his next competition. The hurdle for her to overcome however was made by her and Daniel, as they had both agreed when they began living together, that neither would encroach upon the other's job or life. To her surprise, however, Daniel agreed to accompany the Cardinal for a day or two, as he said it would be an adventure and informative. Evidently, she did have a power over Daniel. After two hours of bed sheet twisting sex, they lay entwined on the damp bed and planned the day. It was only a few hours away actually and Daniel had to make plans of his own.

After the announcement from the Associated Press that the mantis demanded a Black mass and that one was going to be performed at the Cathedral that afternoon, the news media filled the streets, testing the police cordon.

"Daniel Salvino! It's a pleasure to meet you." The Cardinal began. "I saw your last fight here in Chicago. I must say, you were intense. I think you crippled that guy."

"The pleasure is mine Your Emmince." Daniel replied. "I don't' recall the match you refer to."

"You know the one where the red-head, Rachael, the cop, jumped in front of you?" the Cardinal said.

"Oh, yes, I remember that. She was very brave that night and I knew I had to keep her around after that," Daniel replied.

"So, you two are, as we say, an item?"

"I believe that is the correct terminology today. Yes, we're an item. In fact, she insisted that we spend the day together."

"You really think this guy will try to harm me?" the Cardinal asked.

"Well, he's killed two priests, of a sort, and we don't want to take any chances. He lives for attention and if he could use this Black Mass nonsense as a ruse to get to you, he would. So, we'll spend the day together. OK?"

"I warn you, young man, I'm boring." The Cardinal replied.

"Then we're just alike. Rachael says I'm a bore all the time."

"I think she meant boor, Mr. Salvino, as I see you as anything but boring. Let's go then, we have a Black Mass to fake," the Cardinal said as he headed for the door to his impressive office.

With the Traffic Division in complete control of the streets surrounding the Cathedral which is now rote to them, given the number of times they seal the area off for dignitaries visiting the Cathedral and its newly ordained Cardinal, approaching the Cathedral would be difficult.

However, true to the plan and prior experience with the Mantis, the Black Mass was to be videotaped and that required at least one film crew being admitted to the Cathedral inside.

Gibson watched the side door that was open to the "media." The "media," however, who came and went with boxes, bundles and such, were all cops, waiting for Evan to appear.

Evan knew that they would be waiting for him to appear, just as they were at Wriggly Field when he had the White Sox play the Cubs the day he was stabbed by the dirt bag that he made into "road pizza" later on. Evan was listening to the Dark Lord, who commanded him to bring glory to His name. The Cardinal.

Evan discovered, contrary to rational thinking, that the daily schedule of the Cardinal, a public figure and ombudsman for the Church, is generally public information. The rather detailed layout of the Cathedral is open to the public almost twenty-four hours per day.

With the exception of the Black Mass, which was going to be a meeting with a charity group seeking funding, the Cardinal had one speaking engagement at a seminary. Evan knew that approaching the Cathedral would mean facing a plethora of agents and cops. Without question, it would be surrounded by law enforcement, just as Wrigley Field was, in hopes he would expose himself to capture. Once again, however, Evan only needed to see the grip the Mantis maintained on the City of Chicago and its leaders.

Capture meant failure and failure equaled death in an excruciating fashion. Both options, while in the service of the Dark Lord, are unacceptable. In the event that he had stumbled and fell into the waiting hands of law enforcement, Evan very quietly prepared himself for swift departure.

In Wisconsin, one can purchase everything that is required to assemble garden variety bombs. In the hardware stores, you find the plumbing pipe with threated end-caps, black powder and wire. If you know how to ask, you can buy the little caps that will detonate when given an electrical charge. These are used primarily for fireworks, but in reality, are nothing less than blasting caps for explosives.

If you walk to another area of the store, once can find the perfect device for affixing your homemade bomb to the body. A waist trimmer. Those elastic belts with Velcro closures, that fat people use to make them feel trim and fit. Install a few elastic loops to hold the pipes and you have a personalized suicide device.

By some measure of guidance from his Master, Evan had created such a device, with eight inch lengths of two-inch galvanized pipe, packed tightly with "Super X" black powder and two, rectangular, nine volt batteries for power and a simple toggle switch for final judgment time.

Evan hoped to get close enough to the Cardinal, where he could persuade the holy man to accompany him and spare others around them if he were to detonate the device he wore around his waist. All he needed was just a little luck.

Accompanying the Cardinal, now riding in the black limo provided by the Church for such functions, Daniel found himself acting as if he were unaccustomed to such luxury, as they headed to the seminary.

"Where are he headed your Eminence?" Daniel asked.

"Paul, please and we're heading to Skokie, where we'll be surrounded by young men and women who are giving their lives to their faith." The Cardinal replied.

"Will there be a lot of people there? " Daniel asked.

"About a hundred or so, but the press will be there to catch my every word, as they usually do and then use eight seconds of it on the air."

"Do they have security people?" David countered.

"They'll have a couple people to direct traffic. If you're thinking the killer will attack me there, you are very misguided. This Mantis, as I've read anyhow, has targeted those with... shall we say, alternative life styles. I assure you, I am not of that ilk. I am without carnal needs, as God has given me the strength to devote my life to Him only and not a family." The Cardinal pontificated now.

Daniel smiled, as a warrior, he realized the value of surprise and would not let the Cardinal out of his sight, no matter how many speeches he there his way. "Then this will be easy and we'll head back to the Cathedral for the show. Maybe this guy will walk into the trap there that I am certain the police have laid for him."

"Oh, have they. This Black Mass will never happen. I'll never permit such an atrocity upon the Church and the God I love. They're making it look like they're filming and there are hundreds of cops waiting for him to try his luck."

"You think he'll walz into the trap like that?" Daniel asked.

"He demanded this Satanic ritual. How could he resist attending? Of course he'll be there somewhere." The Cardinal said boastfully.

"They didn't catch him at Wrigley Field. What makes you so confident now, if I might ask?"

"Because, God wasn't watching over Wrigley Field that day. Remember, the Cubs lost?" the Cardinal said jokingly.

"We're here, sir," the chauffer said.

"Daniel, please don't embarrass me here. I am among my own kind here. Really. We're safe here." The Cardinal said as the limo parked in front of the lannon-stone building. "Here we go. In and out in a half hour tops."

"Great," Daniel replied as he exited the limo and walked around to open the Cardinal's door, as if he were his attaché'.

The Cardinal was instantly surrounded by media, which made Daniel slightly nervous, followed by a throng of frocked seminarians, all of whom sought his blessing and to kiss his ring.

Once inside the chapel area, Daniel relaxed more and watched the Cardinal give his speech on the tremendous sacrifice each of them were making in the name of God and how he has never regretted his years of service and chastity.

"Bless me your Eminence, for I am about to sin," the seminarian said, His head bowed in reverence.

"And what is your sin, my son," the Cardinal asked from the podium.

"I am about to commit a mortal sin, Your Eminence" Daniel heard him say loudly, wanting the entire room to hear. Without explanation, Daniel came closer to the Cardinal.

"Come here, my son. God will give you the strength to defeat the Devil" the Cardinal replied.

The seminarian took a few steps and stopped short of the Cardinal's position. When he raised his head to face the Cardinal, Daniel knew in an instant who it must be.

Unzipping the robe now, Evan showed the Cardinal the string of shrapnel throwing pipe bombs that surrounded his abdomen. "I am about to kill us all, Your Eminence. The Dark Lord demands the souls of these neophytes around us."

"My son, you don't want to harm these people. It's me that you have come to kill and I do not fear death, as I will be in heaven for eternity. Let these people go," the Cardinal asked.

Daniel could see Evan's red eyes and gnarled hands with long fingernails. He knew that even with his speed, he could not close the distance between himself and Evan before the flip of a switch sent hot shrapnel flying.

"Have you come here to die with me, my son?"

"I am not your son!" Evan shouted. "I am the archangel of the Dark Lord. Satan himself curses you and this Bastian of false prophecy. My Master is coming,"
Evan said loudly, turning slightly, so everyone could hear him. "He is far more powerful than the man you call Jesus, born of a whore named Mary and her aged lover, Joseph, whom she screwed anywhere hay was strewn. The Dark Lord is the real Lord."

"Then what reason brings you here? Why have you come here?" the Cardinal asked.

"Behold all of you, for I am the Mantis. "Evan shouted out. "I am the man who demands a Black Mass. I am the man you fear and the darkness that I carry. Behold people, the emissary of the Dark Lord, Satan himself, in the flesh."

"Satan, why don't you and I walk out of here, alone? These people have not offended you." The Cardinal pleads now.

"you and I have a higher calling, don't we. You and I will die in service to opposing powers." Evan said flatly now, no longer shouting. "You and I embrace death, don't we?"

"Daniel," the Cardinal said, "would you mind opening the door beside you so this man and I can leave here together?"

Looking between the Cardinal and Evan, he realized that the Cardinal was willing to sacrifice himself to save those of the seminary.

"If I am permitted to drive, Your Eminence." Daniel responded.

"Is that all-right with you, Satan? Can my assistant drive us to wherever it is you desire?"

Evan had never seen Daniel and in his loose-fitting slacks and black shirt, looked rather generic in appearance. "Let's head to the coach that will serve as your coffin, priest. Once move, however, and I shall take some of these souls around me, to Hell."

Evan grabbed several of the terrified seminarians from their seats and held them close.

"Lead us not, into temptation, Your Holiness, or we shall face our masters with plenty of company. Let's go. I want to watch the mass." Evan said.

Daniel opened the side door and with several young men and women as a shield, Evan slowly walked to the open door, the Cardinal a few feet in front of him. Once they were free of the seminarians, Daniel hoped to find a way to disarm Evan or incapacitate him, but for the moment, he was helpless.

"You first," Evan said curtly to the Cardinal.

"Let them go." The Cardinal began. "They haven't done you no harm and I promise you, as God is my witness, neither I nor Daniel will try anything and will go freely."

"Daniel, get in the car and close the partition." Evan demanded.

With reluctance and a stern look from the Cardinal, Daniel complied.

"Now, you first" Evan said.

The Cardinal slid across the rear seat, careful not to threaten Evan accidently and Evan sat inside the door.

"Daniel, drive very cautiously to the Cathedral. We don't want the Cardinal late, do we?"

A look in the inside rearview mirror told him to comply with Evan's command and Daniel began to drive. Now, he hoped they wouldn't be spotted by any police patrols, after being alerted from the seminary.

"What do you want with me?" was the last Daniel heard from the Cardinal, as the divider rolled up, giving the two men privacy. Daniel's first inclination was to call Rachael on his cell phone and tell her to have all units back off, but considered involving the woman he loved, in a mad situation with a bomb that could shred her as well.

"Well, I am giving you the opportunity to repent and walk away from this false prophet you represent." Evan said.

"Preposterous. Kill me now, so that I may walk in heaven with my God." The Cardinal replied.

"The Dark Lord is coming. Not like your phony predictions either. He has told me that he comes to claim what is His and take me with him."

"God created this dark angel you call Lord. You are guaranteeing, your soul will spend eternity in hell," the Cardinal argued.

"My Master has shown me his kingdom and it is a wonderful place, not the Lake of Fire your church conjured up in the 1300's after Dante' painted a horned devil to sell paintings," Evan spat out.

"I have no answer for you, my son. You believe in your Master, as I believe in God. We are emissaries, as you will." The Cardinal said, and then continued. "May I ask what your plans are with us?"

"Tell your people that the true Lord is coming soon and give them the chance to save themselves. Give the Black Mass and stop pretending that it will go on as I intended. I assure you, I will harvest many lives if you don't. I want to see news media inside the Cathedral, where the mass is being held and I want a picture of you there, or I shall take a hundred souls to the Dark Lord tonight. Am I perfectly clear, sir?" Evan asked.

"I cannot authorize such a service to be held in the Cathedral. Only His Eminence, the Pope, can do such a thing," the Cardinal replied, as he sought a method to stall Evan's killing innocent people.

"Then I suggest that you begin making calls, or by tonight, you can tell him a hundred people have died because of his stubbornness," Evan replied as he looked out the car windows. "Tell Daniel to get off at Dempster and pull over."

Using the intercom, he relayed Evan's directions to Daniel, who was eager to comply.

As the limo came to a stop, the Cardinal asked who Evan was so that he could pray for him.

"Quentin and I shall ask my Master to spare you from eternal damnation. Remember, a hundred lives will be lost if you continue the charade."

"Go in peace, Quentin. I can feel your pain and suffering. Go in peace," the Cardinal said.

Evan opened the rear door and slid to the edge of the seat. "Remember, people are counting on you." Evan said then, after a brief pause continued, "And tell Daniel to call Rachael and tell her he's all- right. I can smell her on him, which tells me that he's not a priest, but her lover or a cop. He saved your life this afternoon, Mr. Holy man."

The Cardinal breathed a sigh of relief when Evan stepped from the limo and headed for a crowd of people.

Daniel did not even consider giving pursuit as he watched Evan blend into the people, his seminary frock giving him the spiritual appearance. His job was to protect the Cardinal, who was safe in the rear seat of the limo, not apprehend bombers in crowds of people.

"Daniel, can you get us the hell out of here?" the Cardinal said, before realizing that he used the word "hell" in his request and a smile appeared on his face.

"Where to?"

"The Cathedral, please. And call Rachael. Tell her to clear the area. We might have a bomb inside the Cathedral." The Cardinal responded, as he looked out the rear window forlornly.

"Rach, it's me," Daniel said into his cell phone, "listen to me, we're OK but there could be a bomb in the Cathedral,"

The Cardinal could not hear Rachael's responses on the other end of the call, as his mind was intensely focused on the decision regarding the Black Mass and Evan's promise of a hundred lives.

"Yes, I'm sure it was your Mantis character. We'll be there shortly and you can have your forensics people take the car."

"Daniel," the Cardinal said, "he knew."

"He knew about you and Rachael. Said he could smell her all over you and that either you were her lover or a cop," the Cardinal said flatly.

"What?" Daniel exclaimed. "There is no way for him to link her and I. He was guessing, that's all."

"No, Daniel, he said that you saved my life this afternoon. I think he likes her in some way," the Cardinal replied.

As the rage ran unchecked in Daniel's mind, a sensation, he never permits as it clouds the thought processes, he pushed the accelerator pedal to the floor. He had the need to see her safe and protect her now, as the Cardinal was safe.

As the limo neared the Loop, marked squad cars, lights flashing, surrounding the car and escorted it through the heavy traffic as if the President were on-board. By the time the entourage of vehicles arrived a the Cathedral, approximately a dozen cars were involved, making quite a scene for media cameras and people on the expressway.

When Daniel spotted Rachael, a radio in her hand, standing in the middle of the now empty street, as if she were a gunfighter, Daniel smiled.

The Cardinal rushed from the limo and headed directly inside the Cathedral. Everyone knew that it would be fruitless to try to prevent him from going inside. In a flurry of black and red robes, the Cardinal disappeared. He had to tell the Pope what he just encountered and the evil that threatened innocent lives.

"Your Eminence" the call began, "I just met Satin himself," the Cardinal said into his desk phone as he began to call.

Chapter 14

"Ben," Rachael shouted as she ran into his office, "we got a hit."

Ori had been on a call when she blew into his office and quickly said good-bye and hung up. "On who, Rachael?"

"Him, Ben the Mantis. His name is Evan Felder," she gushed.

"The lab guys do it or the feds?" Ben replied.

"Don't ask how we have it. That's all I can say. I pulled his driver's license picture and it's him, Ben. He lives in Wheaton."

"Get SWAT and have them meet us on the way. I'll call Gillings and let him know. You have an address?" Ben asked excitedly.

"Here I'll call SWAT and meet you out front," Rachael blurted and was off in a flash.

"Calvin, we have a hit on this Mantis character. Run the name Evan Felder, that's E-V-A-N- F-E-L-D-E-R and show Gibson the photo. Guy lives in Wheaton and we're on our way there now with SWAT." Ben said with authority.

With sirens screaming, the cavalcade of cars and vans sped west towards Wheaton, which was normally an hour drive, but with Rachael at the wheel, would be about one-half the time now.

They were joined by Gibson and Perzigaian, just about at O'Hare and the expressway, who was in contact via cell phone with Rachael.

The address in Wheaton was registered to Mr. and Mrs. Evan Felder and the team planned to descend on the home, without involving Wheaton Police for risk to drawing too much attention and tipping their hands.

Silently, having parked their vehicles some distance from the home, the assembly of feds and C.P.D. officers stealthily approached the home. Seeing no sign of Evan, but seeing a woman unloading groceries from the trunk of her car, the officers closed.

Rachael, clad in a wind breaker, which covered her body armor, approached the woman. "Mrs. Felder?" She asked, while looking around.

Startled at the sight of Rachael, her Glock held at her side, dropped her bag of groceries back into the trunk. "Yes, you scared me. Who are you?"

"Police. Is your husband around?" Rachael asked the frightened woman.

"No. Evan hasn't been around here for some time. Ever since he..." she replied.

"Since when Mrs. Felder?" Rachael asked, her hand still holding her Glock.

"Since he got sick. What do you want with Evan? Is he hurt or something?"

"Mind if we look inside, Mrs. Felder? Just routine and we won't bother a thing" Rachael asked politely.

"Well, I don't see why you'd want to do such a thing, but satisfy your curiosity. Evan isn't here" the woman said angrily now.

With a simple nod, the other members closed on the home, entering the front door, weapons readied and aimed in front of them now.

Holstering her Glock. Rachael asked the woman, "What do you mean 'sick' Mrs. Felder?"

"I don't want to discuss it. It's Evan's personal life and all. Why are you so interested? And why are so many of you here, with all those guns and outfits?"

"Clean, Sergeant" a male voice said as a number of SWAT members excited the home.

"Thanks guys. Let's look around and see if he....was here recently. Rachael directed. She almost said "butchered people here recently" but held her tongue.

"Will do" the SWAT leader said in response.

"Mrs. Felder, can we talk inside?" Rachael asked, now joined by Gibson and Ben.

"I guess. The neighbors are going to talk about this something terrible though" she responded.

"I'm sorry about that Mrs. Felder. Can we help you with those?" Rachael asked, nodding at the bags of groceries to her male counterparts.

"Mrs. Felder, do you have any idea where we can find your husband? Can we talk to him?" Gibson asked.

"And who are you?"

"I'm with the FBI Ma'am, I'm sorry. Here" He said showering her his credentials.

"FBI? What did Evan do that you want to talk to him?" she asked Gibson.

"Ma'am, we can't discuss the investigation. We-just need to talk to your husband. Can you arrange that?" Gibson replied.

"Wish I could talk to Evan. God I miss him. He went off to..." she trailed off.

"When he went off to what, Mrs. Felder," Rachael asked, woman to woman.

"Evan is sick. Very sick," the wife replied.

You mean psychologically, Mrs. Felder?" Ben asked in his baritone voice.

Mrs. Felder eyed Ben before asking. "You FBI, too?"

"No Ma'am, I'm Lieutenant Ori, Chicago P.D." Ben said, extending his badge case carrying his gold star and photo ID.

"Evan must be in real trouble, with all you people here," the woman said as she collapsed into a chair and put her hands to her face, weeping. "He's dying! My husband is dying. You satisfied now?"

Sitting beside her now, Rachael asked her softly, "Dying from what Mrs. Felder?"

Through the sobs, the woman replied, "Some damn tumor in his head. Doctors said they couldn't cut it out or it'd kill him."

"When was the last time you saw Evan?" Gibson asked now.

Sniffling, the distraught woman said, "he stopped by to see how we were doing. He looked terrible. He's not the same man I married. That damn thing in his head is killing him slowly."

"Was this recently, Mrs. Felder?" Rachael asked.

"A few days ago. He looked terrible. He didn't want us to watch him die, so he just took off."

"Mrs. Felder" Rachael began, "how did Evan discover the tumor?"

"The headaches" she replied. "And the nightmares, too", she added.

"Nightmares?" Rachael asked.

"Yes, he would carry on so and scream while I held him. They must have frightened him."

"Did these nightmares always happen?" Rachael asked again.

"No, in the past couple months, maybe six months, I'd say. Awful." She answered.

"Is this when the tumor was diagnosed?" Gibson asked now.

"No, before he had the headaches. He'd shake violently and scream out a name and grow silent again."

"A name, Mrs. Felder?" Ben asked.

"Quentin. I think something happened between them," they answered, almost whispering at the end.

"Did he ever shout Quentin's last name?"

"Of course not. Besides, he told me about the bully from high school, when we were dating."

"Do you have a recent photo of your husband, Mrs. Felder?" Gibson enquired.

"Nothing you can use, I'm afraid. When he was here, he looked nothing like the man I married. Sorry."

The wife looked haggard when everyone departed. The locals, who had finally been brought up to speed on the situation, agreed to place uniform cars out front, twenty four hours per day.

Having Evan's name, gave Rachael the idea to exploit a vulnerability and shake the Mantis's foundation. Later that afternoon, with the help of the Associated Press, every media outlet carried the photograph from Evan's driver's license and a plea for information on the whereabouts of Evan Felder, also known as the Mantis.

Vulnerable and wounded from the discovery of his true identity, Rachael hoped for him to make a mistake.

Chapter 15

"Khoren," Gibson said, getting the attention of his partner, who was reading some report. "Hey! Khoren!" he repeated louder.

"Huh?" Khoren responded but still not giving Gibson his undivided attention.

"Rachael and I had sex last night," Gibson said.

"What did you just say?" Khoren said with a start, his attention on his partner now, his eyes wide open.

"I said, I ran that Quentin kid and there's a warrant for him."

"That's not what you said." Khoren returned.

"Of course it is. You think I have dreams of Rachael or something?" Gibson volleyed back.

Wondering, now if he really heard something about Rachael, Khoren decided to let it pass. "What about this guy?"

"We have a warrant for failure to report for duty, which means he chickened out after being sworn in and took off." Gibson said.

"Does he still have family?" Khoren asked his attention on "full alert" now.

"I checked. Parents are in their seventies, but still alive, evidentially. Ran their address through the Registrar of Deeds for Du Page County and the home is still in their names. Seems that they're older, but alive.

"I think we should interview them" Khoren suggested.

"I'm already signing us out for Wheaton, Illinois."

"I'll drive" Khoren said, more as a directive than a suggestion.

"Why's that?"

"Because, I want to get there without dying along the way, or hurting someone. Every time we get close to making an arrest, you seem to get wild."

"I'm hurt Khoren. Really hurt, that you would say something like that to me" Gibson mused.

"Have you forgotten Miami, partner? You know, that little boat chase that brought us here in the first place?"

"That was not my fault! I was making a legal arrest and I had to use that boat to prevent the subject from escaping." Gibson replied while getting his jacket on.

"The Coast Guard was waiting for him, Hollywood. He had nowhere to run." Khoren returned as they were readying for their trip west of Chicago where Quentin's parents live.

"Khoren, how would I know that asshole would drive that boat into the man's kitchen?"

"Because, brother, you ran him off the road or waterway, whatever they call it and pushed the main into that house" Khoren fired back.

"You done? I mean, are you done grilling me over one slight miscalculation?"

"That miscalculation, brother, cost the Bureau three million dollars" Khoren said with a smile across his face now.

"They had the Marshals pay that out of assets that we seize and turn over to them. So, the taxpayer never felt a thing. Drug dealers did" Gibson returned as they headed out the door.

"You think that makes it OK then? What about the owner of the boat you demolished and buried in that man's kitchen?" Khoren asked now.

"Khoren, the man is the quarterback for the New England Patriots. He is more than what that stupid boat cost in a single game. "Gibson replied.

"Oh, so that Mr. FBI Agent, gives you the right to swipe it and destroy it? Because he makes more in a single football game than what we make in our lives as agents?" Khoren asked, as they entered the parking garage and headed for his squad car.

"Khoren, he got a new toy boat and personal letter from the Director for allowing the use of his boat during the apprehension of violent felons in flight."

As they exited the federal building on Dearborn Street and turned left, Khoren said, "I have a bad feeling about this case, man."

"What's that mean, Khoren?"

"It means that I think this Felder is different somehow. I think it's going to end bad." Khoren replied, all joking around aside.

"Khoren, don't let his guy's bullshit get to you. He's not a Mantis for real. The media made that up and because it's catchy, it stuck. This guy is just another man who decided to kill people for recreation."

"Listen, Gibson, for just once, listen. I'm telling you that I feel something is very different with this guy and I don't mean just psychologically, either."

"Don't get spooked, Khoren." Gibson returned.

"I'm not spooked you asshole. I'm saying that I can feel the difference. Something or some force is at play here." Khoren explained.

"He's not the Devil, Khoren. He is not employed by Satan, either. He's a man. A man with a tumor in his head, that'll kill him before trial and is driving him to murder people."

"There is something very, very wrong with this case. I'm telling you this because I want you to tell my wife if..." Khoren ended.

"Khoren, we're going to take this guy down, just like any other arrest. He'll start crying when we put the cuffs on him." Gibson said, trying to reassure his partner and himself, as well.

Gibson shared the same feeling about the Mantis case. As they progressed towards an arrest, he too had begun to wonder about a killer that would do what he did to people and not have some evil mechanic driving him.

"Let's see what this guy's family says about him. I just wanted you to know how I feel. Something isn't right about this case. That's all." Khoren replied as they headed west on the expressway.

It was a silent ride to Wheaton after the initial conversation, as both men contemplated their similar feelings about the case and how it would end.

Pulling up in front of a now dilapidated clapboard house in grave need of a coat of paint, Khoren said, "According to the GPS, this is it. Looks like the Aadams family lives here."

"They're old, Khoren. They can't crawl up ladders to paint and their son took off from the Army, so he's not going to help them," Gibson replied, trying to sound convincing.

The home was "neglected," as one would say best describes the house. Weeds grew where flower beds once existed; the partially buried bricks attesting to the time spend on defining them. The lawn would make for an excellent "before" picture for either a grass service or heavy duty lawn mower, as the mustard colored flowers were almost knee high and made the front of the house resemble a pasture, more than a lawn.

Approaching the front door, apprehensive of the tensile strength of the boards making up the stairs leading up to the porch, the agents stopped and looked at each other.

Between them was a "dust devil," its cyclonic wind, spiraling upward, carrying tiny bits of debris, like its big brother. Dust devils are seen all the time in arid climates like Arizona and Texas, but they are quite rare in Illinois. The agents watched the tiny tornado rise and fall, eventually disappearing into nothingness and the tiny tidbits fell to the sidewalk.

"Who the hell lives here? The Dark Knight?" Gibson joked.

"Let's just interview these people about their son and get back to work, shall we?" Khoren replied.

After carefully padding up the creaking steps, the men stood at the front door, which now opened to reveal an elderly lady in a happy print sundress and huge smile. "Can I help you fellas?" She asked.

"Yes, Ma'am, we're with the FBI and would like to talk to you about your son, Quentin" Khoren said, as he held his ID open for her to examine.

"Oh, he doesn't live here anymore. He joined the Army and made a life for himself elsewhere, I suppose," she answered forlornly.

"May we come inside, Ma'am?" Khoren asked.

"I haven't tidied up yet this morning" she demurred.

"We really need to talk to you" Gibson interjected.

"Well, I suppose being FBI I can trust you" she said as she unlatched the door.

"Thank you" Khoren said as he opened the door and stepped inside.

Unlike the exterior, the interior of the home was immaculate. Everything, although a bit excessive from years of collecting memorabilia, was pristine and clean. Tables were dust free and the living room smelled of lilacs.

"You have a very nice home," Khoren said.

"Dad can't take care of the outside like he used to, got arthritis now, but we manage."

"Where is your husband, Ma'am? Is he home?" Gibson asked.

"Let me tell him we have company. He's down in the basement tinkering on something. That man is always tinkering on some gadget or electronic thing," she said as she shuffled off.

Khoren began examining the photos on the walls. For a life time of family memories, there was but one of a much younger wife, holding an infant.

"That's Quentin at six months" Khoren heard behind him. Dad's on his way up from his workshop."

"Thank you" Khoren replied. "Do you have any recent photos of your son?"

"After he joined the Army, we never heard from him again. Oh my, he isn't one of those 'missing in action' people or hurt is he?" the woman asked, genuine concern on her face.

"We have no knowledge of either, Ma'am. To our knowledge, we have no information that anything has happened to him." Khoren replied.

The last few steps from the basement were easily heard and a moment later, an elderly man with white, close cut hair and square jaw, appeared.

"FBI, huh?" the man said as he walked into the room. "Kid must have done something big this time. What'd he do? Rob a bank? Rape an old woman, maybe?"

"Sir, my partner would like to interview you, while I speak with your wife. You know, that's how we feds do things and all. But, we have no knowledge of Quentin doing anything. We're here for background information only. OK?" Khoren asked.

"Is he involved in some secret shit and you're doing a background investigation?" the father asked.

"Sir, we're not at liberty to discuss why we're here, you know that." Gibson interjected, picking up on his partner's lead and the man's assumptions.

"Oh, yeah, sure. Ah, you want to see my workshop?" the father asked.

"Actually, sir, I was going to ask you if I could see it. I'll bet it's like Tim the tool man Taylor's shop, huh?" Gibson said as he followed the man back the way he had come. Both agents had perked up when they heard about a workshop, as they knew Quentin or Evan or someone called the mantis, needed a special place to do their grizzly work.

When Gibson and the father disappeared, Khoren asked, "Ma'am, can we sit down?"

"Oh my, sure, please." She said and daintily sat on the edge of the couch.

"May I record this? It's easier than my trying to take notes and we can just talk then. OK?"

"Oh, my, that does make sense." She answered.

After setting his cell phone between them, Khoren began by stating the date, time, location and names of everyone present for the interview.

"Ma'am, I'm here for background information only, on your son, Quentin. When was the last time you saw him?"

"When he went off to fight for his country" she said proudly. "I'll bet he looks handsome in his uniform too. Probably a general by now, isn't he?"

"Ma'am, I can't answer that," Khoren explained, then continued. "you saw him leave for the Army?"

The hesitation struck him as odd.

"Not exactly" she said hesitantly.

"Would you mind explaining that, please?" Khoren asked politely.

Meanwhile, in the basement, where Gibson discovered a workshop far superior to anything that Tim Allen even envisioned for his show, he was stoically shown the inner work of a man who was meticulous in planning.

"Sir, did Quentin work or spend time with you down here?" Gibson enquired.

"That boy wasn't interested in working with his hands like a man. He always had other ideas for himself."

"Well, sir, when he joined the Army, did that surprise you?" Gibson countered. "After all, defending his country is pretty tough to do."

The man looked at Gibson carefully, as if he were studying him. "We signed the papers so he could join up and get outta this place. He was..."

"He was...different, that's all." The man answered and began to show Gibson his latest project.

"What do you mean, 'different' sir?"

"Look, Mr. FBI, I ain't proud of what Quentin is, but happy he found a life for himself in the Army."

"Sir, I don't understand what you mean by 'what he is'? What exactly does that mean?" Gibson asked while looking at a cordless drill with "Milwaukee" written on it.

"Look, a father doesn't like saying such things. It hurts, ya know? My son, is gay or queer, however you call it today. In my day, we called them queers, but that ain't politically correct nor more. Right?"

"You think that's why your son joined the Army? Because he's gay?" Gibson asked.

"That boy's a 'meat grazer'. Know what that is, Mr. FBI?"

"No sir, what does that mean to you?"

"He liked looking at other boys. He looked at the dicks and balls, Mr. FBI. You understand now?"

"I'm sorry, but I have to know these things and I assure you, it's not going to be made public information." Gibson returned.

Looking into Gibson's eyes, as if he could see if he were lying to him, the father continued. "He told me he had a small dick, once and when I asked him how he knew such things he said that he saw the sizes of the others in the shower. Sick, huh?"

"And what did you say to him?" Gibson asked.

"I told him to quit looking at the other guys like they were meat and act like a man."

"And he did, right?" Gibson enquired.

"Boy left town, Mr. FBI, cause someone would have killed him if he didn't, I'm sure." The man said and looked at Gibson a moment before going on. "He deserted, didn't he?"

"Sir, I can't discuss why we're here. We'd like to talk to him." Gibson responded officially.

"I used to find those queer books under his bed. Know how that makes a man feel? To learn that his son, might be screwing another man like an 'Ass Pirate', Mr. FBI?"

"Did anything specific happen here before Quentin left?" Gibson asked.

They sat on a stool and looked at the tools neatly laid out on the work bench. "Quentin was a bully. He liked the younger kids. He could impress them and all. Know what I mean?"

"I'm not sure, sir." Gibson said tactfully.

"I received a call once. Some guy who claimed Quentin exposed himself to his son and supposedly asked his son to hold his dick for him. I told the man his son was sick for saying some shit like that and hung up on him. But later, I could sense that the boy probably did that, or worse and was sick to my stomach. Told Quentin to get the fuck outta our lives; leave us alone."

"And when he wanted to enlist, you were happy to sign the papers." Gibson replied.

"Absolutely. I think he did something really bad before he left here" the man said cautiously.

"Any idea what that might have been sir?"

"Not exactly. He never came right out and said he done something to some boy, but I think he might a raped some boy or made him…suck on him. If you know what I mean." The man said while he looked down at the gnarled wooden top of his work bench after years of fixing things or building projects.

"So you never heard from your son again, after he left town for the Army?"

"A buddy told me he saw Quentin in a bar, night before he left. Said the owner told him that if he was old enough to die for his country, he was old enough to drink there. I guess the boy got pretty drunk, as the owner poured shots for him as a going away present to a soldier" the man answered.

"Sir, if you hear from Quentin, would you mind calling either my partner or I? We really need to ask him a few questions" Gibson said in his most professional voice.

"I will, but that boy ain't calling here. He was happy to leave this house."

As Gibson, leaving the man to the solitude his workshop afforded him entered the living room as Khoren was talking with the wife.

"Well, thank you Ma'am, for spending time with me. Remember, if you hear from your son, give us a call. We have some questions for him. OK?" Khoren asked as he rose and headed for the front door.

"I will. You boys have a nice day now" she said as she quietly closed the door behind them.

Once in the sanctuary of the squad car assigned to Khoren, it was Gibson who spoke first.

"I'm going to call the BAU when we get back. I gotta hunch about all this."

"What'd the father tell you? Anything of value?" Khoren asked.

"The man was full of disgust and hatred for his own son. Says Quesntin was gay and might have done something really bad before joining the Army."

"You think Quentin might be Evan or something?" Khoren enquired.

"That might explain a lot, Khoren. Why our guy has targeted gays. There's a pretty strong motive. Maybe Quentin raped him. The father says that was just one possibility." Gibson responded.

"You better let Rachael know what's happening out here. Don't want her pissed at us any more than she is already." Khoren stated.

"What's she pissed about?" Gibson replied.

"Because you never let her know about finding Quentin's folks and were coming here to interview them."

"How does she know that? We haven't…, he looked at Khoren as he trailed off his sentence.

"She called me and I told her where we were and how wonderful his folks were." Khoren said with a smile.

"Says you're an asshole for not letting her know, so she would be here too."

"Damn, was all Gibson replied? He knew he was in for a tongue lashing from her and probably deserved it.

Chapter 16

Arrest warrants are based on "probable cause," which presents as a sophisticated legal term with an elusive definition. Truth behold, the simple definition that was coined by the Supreme Court is that one must determine if a crime was committed and probably by a particular defendant or defendants.

Prosecutors prepare the documents for a judge or magistrate to sign, authorizing arrests. Prosecutors are not at liberty to sign arrests warrants, which is often times misadventure by the unknowledgeable.

"Good morning Sergeant Hart. He's waiting for you, so go on in. He's got coffee, too" the receptionist at the Cook County State's Attorney's Office said, as Rachael walked, carrying several folders and binders.

"Thank you," was all Rachael said, walking past, as she had an appointment with the State's Attorney himself.

The "Criminal Courts: building for Cook County, where Chicago is located, is an old building situated on the corners of California and 26th Avenues. A monolith to justice for all, the building, despite nominal reconstruction and remolding, is not the stereotypical building that one envisions.

"I hope you don't mind meeting in here?" The Chief Prosecutor asked when he intercepted her as she headed for his office.

Your office, sir, is barely larger than mine and far more cluttered, so yes, this will do nicely" she joked. It was an accurate statement, that for the head of the largest prosecutor's office in Illinois, you would expect to find an opulent office, resplendant with ornate book shelves and judicial statuary. Instead, he has   room for an executive desk, two chairs, a small credenza and his office chair, barely larger than Rachael's office.

The conference room, on the other hands, where the two were meeting, fits the image of being a haven for the defenders of justice. Ornate, is a word that is generally reserved for intricate carvings, exotic woods and finishes, subdued lighting and an array of books with titles only legal scholars fathom. That is exactly the appearance of the conference room the chief prosecutor wished was his office and not used by every assistant under his stead.

"So, we're ready for a warrant, are we?" he asked her after handing her a steaming cup of coffee and holding her chair for her.

"You are always such a gentleman, sir, the ladies must find you irresistible" Rachael mused as she sipped her coffee.

"If I were younger, Sergeant, I might challenge that man you're so attached to, but I'm an old warhorse now and my days of romping in green pastures are long gone."

"You flatter me, but I think your days are more dedicated to your craft" she replied.

"True, very true. I serve the people of Cook County, which brings us to why you're here. The Mantis case, as I understand it. We're ready to charge someone finally?" He asked, while rolling up the sleeves of his shirt, just beneath his elbows and picked up his pen to make notes.

"His name is Evan Felder. We have positive DNA match and confession to the Cardinal himself, along with one Daniel Salvino."

The prosecutor scribbled some notes on a yellow legal pad and picked up the phone and called his secretary. "OK, send them on in and we'll need you and at least two typists," he said before setting the phone back in the cradle.

Within minutes, the conference room was full of people, including two Assistant States Attorneys, one of whom was the Chief of Felony Crimes, a man she saw frequently on television during major criminal trials and death penalty cases. They were joined by a wave of females for short-hand, document preparation and a Paralegal for organizing the file.

"OK, let's start from the top, shall we? Everybody know each other? This is Sergeant Rachael Hart of the Homicide Division. Her boss, by the way, is a man named Ori and is far worse than I to work with," he said jokingly.

After perfunctory introductions, the man who would actually try Evan Felder was, as she had guessed, was the chief of the felony division and not the State's Attorney. Instead, the State's Attorney would make a cameo appearance; woo the jury with his well-publicized examination of a witness, before leaving the courtroom for an interview before the cameras outside.

The paralegal, who sat to Rachael's left would tag every document and catalog it on an official form, before handing it to the Assistant State's Attorney who would seek the death penalty for American's most voracious and noteworthy killer, to date, surpassing the "BTK" killer.

For two hours, Rachael presented documents, reports, photos and other pieces of evidence that would be referred to in her Affidavit, which would then accompany the Warrant, as they approached the Chief Judge for his signature on a document that would become one of the most sought after pieces of macular memorabilia.

Once Rachael provided the documents and her version of the crime, the people would then part to prepare the Warrant, her Affidavit, Search Warrants for the Wheaton home where he lived and the office he worked in downtown, as well as for the medical records from the neurosurgeon and any other who has treated Evan Felder. Each knows their assigned tasks and at the end, a sheaf of papers will be generated, signed by the States Attorney, herself and the Chief Judge, prior to disclosure to the media that was gathering outside after receiving an anonymous tip.

"Can you tell me how you obtained the DNA match, Sergeant?" the States Attorney asked, using her rank as the interview was being recorded electronically and by stenographic means.

"Our technicians obtained a DNA profile from the insurance company Mr. Felder obtained life insurance through, in case he were to meet his end in a fashion where identification became necessary for payment or a denial of benefits, " she replied.

Holding a finger up, which halted the recording of further conversation, the States Attorney asked "Rachael, did we subpoena these records or DNA profile?"

"No sir," was all she said.

Her answer called for a private consultation between the attorneys, where it was mutually decided to avoid further questioning regarding how the DNA profile was obtained.

"You said you also have a confession from Mr. Felder to the Cardinal?" he asked her.

"Yes, while he held the Cardinal and Mr. Salvino hostage with what appeared to be a bomb strapped around his waist, Mr. Felder, who Mr. Salvino personally identified from a photo array of eight similar men, Mr. Felder admitted to being the Mantis and killings" she replied in her most professional fashion.

"Is there any way that you can see, after taking the statements from the Cardinal and Mr. Salvino where Mr. Felder believed he was confessing to the Cardinal as a priest?" The States Attorney asked.

Rachael was well aware of the privilege that exists between a priest and a confessor, which is protected by the constitutional directives. Any defense attorney worth their weight in rock salt would file their motion to exclude Evan's statements to the Cardinal under such constrictions. "No sir, I don't believe , given the method of taking the Cardinal hostage, along with advising him of coming of the Dark Lord, would remotely qualify as a protected confession for evidentiary purposes." She answered.

"And Mr. Salvino was a party to these admissions by Mr. Felder?"

She knew where this question would undeniably lead, as the inclusion of non-clergy to the confession would legally nullify any perceived privilege that a defense attorney could muster. "He was not a direct party to the conversations but as the driver for the Cardinal, overheard everything.

"Let me ask you this, Sergeant. Did you inspect the limo after it was brought to the police impound?" he asked her.

"Yes sir, I was there when our Forensics people went over the car and obtained samples for testing in the lab," she returned.

"Was there a 'privacy curtain' installed in that limo?"

"Yes, sir there was and it was retracted when we took it into custody" she answered.

Again, the States Attorney halted recording. "You know, a first year law student could eat us alive with you you've told me thus far? We've got a DNA profile that was most likely obtained unlawfully and violating God knows how many federal statutes protecting Privacy Act rights. Then, we have a questionable 'confession' to the

Cardinal, as a man of the cloth and the driver simply over-heard. We'll deal with the defense motions that are sure to follow any arrest, but I want you to get me concrete evidence, Sergeant. I want the smoking gun or dripping knife, as the case may be. Am I abundantly clear?"

"Does this mean we're not going after a warrant?" she asked.

"Not at all. I admire your police work in bringing us this guy. Just find me irrefutable evidence when the son of a bitch is arrested. OK?" the States Attorney asked, with heads nodding all around the room.

"I am thoroughly, if nothing else people and I assure you, that I will tie every loose end, cross every T and dot every I. Am I clear here?" she fired back.

"Rachael, we're not questioning your ethics here. We're concerned with technical matters that defense counsel will employ to get their client off or to avoid the death penalty. I believe all of us here have seen your work in the past and have faith in you and your abilities." The States Attorney said.

"Absolutely," The Felony Chief interposed. "You and I have worked before, but the cases never went to trial. That's because your work is thorough and the defendants knew they would probably lose. In fact, I have used your name and reputation to intimidate defense attorneys, so I know your value.

"Thank you. I just wanted to make it clear that I am not slipshod in my methods or easily attacked for credibility. I catch the bad guys. The worst of the bad guys, actually." Rachael said as she looked at everyone seated at the conference table."

"I don't ask for praise or recognition, but I will not tolerate an assault on my character, work ethos or honesty."

A pregnant pause hung in the air like a heavy fog over a pond, and then was removed by the States Attorney who signaled the resuming of the recordings.

"Sergeant Hart, is it your sworn testimony here, that as a result of your training, experience and personal knowledge of this case, that Evan Felder is guilty of the offenses of murder, kidnapping and torture of the victims in this case?"

"It is, sir," she replied.

"Then that concludes this interview," the States Attorney said formally and without another signal, the recordings stopped and a number of the females silently departed the room, each having their respective tasks to perform.

"How about you join me for lunch in my office? While we have lunch, everyone can get the documents prepared and filed. Then, we'll pay a visit to the Chief Judge, who will sign the Warrants and we'll face the media together?" the States Attorney asked.

"I have to call Ben and tell him what's going on. I'll grab a sandwich downstairs and meet you back here. OK?" she replied.

The wizened prosecutor and savvy politician knew that he had offended her, although unintentional for that, he would pay a price. The first installment was the denial of a simple lunch, where he had ordered sandwiches for them.

Rachael enjoyed her quiet lunch in the busy cafeteria located in the basement. She spend almost a half hour on the phone with Ben, where she explained the concerns of the prosecutors and the threat, or implied threat, that she had better present them with admissible evidence that irrefutably convicts the Mantis and sends him to death row.

"We interrupt this broadcast for breaking news. A few minutes ago, the Cook County State's Attorney issued a statement that it had secured an arrest warrant for the man associated with the Mantis slayings." The anchorwoman intoned.

"Son of a bitch! You couldn't wait would you?" she said to herself as she dropped the remnants of her sandwich back onto the paper plate and joined all the other patrons in watching the breaking news.

"Although the States Attorney, pictured here from earlier footage, refused to give the name of the man now being sought, he has stated that the wanted man is from Wheaton, this quiet community west of Chicago."

"Cleaver aren't you, you bastard. You don't say his name, but give up the home city so he knows we are after him. Nice, you son of a bitch!" Rachael said a bit too loud as she tossed her food into the garbage can not far away from her. "Goddamn you."

In the Squad car now, speeding back to Headquarters, she called Ben and told him to turn on the news. "Damn him, Ben. He's alerted this guy that we're onto him and he's going to hide or run on us now."

"He's a politician Rachael. He wins his office by getting the votes and breaking news like this so he's the hero. We just find them and bring them in, so relax." Ben advised.

"It pisses me off, Ben. We work hard at this and me makes it even harder. He should have just said Felder's name and got it over with."

"Rachael, we...," Ben began.

"Hold on Ben, I got the FBI calling me now. I'll see you in a few minutes" she said before switching over to the incoming call from Gibson.

"I know you had nothing to do with disclosing that we know, who our killer is, right?" Gibson asked.

"You know better. That man's an asshole and has just risked people's lives with letting Felder know we're on his ass," she fired back.

Gibson chuckled. "The States Attorney is elected, so he needs the publicity. The U.S. Attorney is appointed by the President and accepted by Congress. See the difference?"

"Yeah, we work for glory hounds and this one just upped the ante on getting this guy without anyone else getting hurt, including us, I might add."

"All that aside, Rachael, we need to coordinate our efforts to get this guy. We promised you it's your case, but all of us here are ready to jump at your command." Gibson said seriously.

"Let's get together at my office and figure out how we split this up and find Felder before he runs on us," she responded.

"You there now?"

"In about ten minutes, I will be" she answered.

"I'll be waiting for you. I'll bring hot coffee too" he said as he disconnected the call.

She had to admit that her first impression of Special Agent Melvin Gibson, was less than stellar. In fact, she detested him. However, she has come to realize that he is a dedicated officer and not really a boor, as he first thought of him. He had kept his word regarding her having the lead role on the case and not trying to take it away from her, despite Felder's crossing state lines to commit more murders. He even amused her now, an unfamiliar emotion between feds and locals.

While Rachael and Gibson were speeding to meet each other to discuss the capture of the Mantis, Evan sat silently in the Jeep as he listened to the special report on the SUV's radio. When the radio host related the hometown of Wheaton, Evan knew, unequivocally, that somehow he had slipped up and was the man they were hunting.

"Master, I have failed thee" Evan said in a whisper, as he looked into the rearview mirror and saw his reflection. The aging had progressed and the wrinkles around his eyes and on his brow had deepened, resembling troughs, not lines, as they etched his flesh. His teeth were yellowed and his eyes were like rubies now. Had the media been provided with his picture, no one would recognize the weathered old man, with claw like hands, as the most depraved killer ever recorded.

Parking in an open meadow in Winfield, a small city adjacent to Wheaton, Evan underwent what can only be labeled as a "Psychotic episode, " as he reeled back and forth from images of him being raped, feeling the searing pain at being penetrated by another man, to being the rapist himself. The images flashed on the silver screen that made up his psyche and he was powerless to make them stop. Vacillating from victim to rapist, he was effectively divided, rendering him little more than a heap of mumbling flesh.

The pain was reaching crescendo limits as if something was crushing his skull in a vice-like grip and strong enough to tear gold from rocks. He needs no further evidence that his Master is upset with him and commands retribution.

When Rachael pulled up front of Headquarters, as promised, Gibson awaited her with large cups of coffee in hand.

"Come on Mr. FBI, we have some work to do. That is the way they pay us the big bucks, right?" she asked striding for the elevators.

"Way to go, Serge," she heard as she walked through the double doors, but did not respond.

"Gibson, let me ask you a question, since you've got his keenly trained federal mind. Where do you think Felder will go?" she asked, then sipped her coffee and sat on the edge of her desk.

Even in a royal blue pants suit, with a slightly lavender shirt, she was nothing short of stunning and the maleness in him could feel the stirrings of desire to have her, which he quickly repressed. "What the hell does that mean?"

"It means I have an idea where we will eventually find out killer, but I want to hear what a finely trained product of Quantico believes." She replied.

"What are you getting at Rachael?"

"Come on Mr. FBI. I have a call to make and I want you to listen" she answered and led him to a small conference room.

Once she had Felder's neurosurgeon on the line, she reminded him who she was, that Gibson was there and that she had a Search Warrant from the chief Judge, to seize his files on Evan Felder.

"So, why are you calling, officer? I have patients here" the doctor answered, annoyed at the intrusion.

Let's stay in the hypothetical, shall we doctor?" she began. "If a person had an inoperable tumor deep inside his brain, could the pain from such a tumor make a victim psychotic?"

"Strictly hypothetical, mind you, a tumor that continues to progress in size, will begin to displace the cranial contents, including the brain and the fluid that helps protect it. When this displacement occurs, the pressure derived from the displacement and the fixed area inside the cranium, the patient will undergo increasing pain. A chronic pain more than likely, but will have its sedentary moments, as well as its intense moments. The chronic suffering by the patients could make him or her suffer psychosis or psychotic episodes, where he would exhibit rage or become violent. Of course, now you're reaching a field of practice, where I am not licensed. Any other questions or may I return to my patients before they become psychotic."

"During these psychotic episodes, doctor, are these victims or patients in control of themselves?" she asked.

"Well, again, this is starting to metamorph from the physiological to the psychological, where I have no expertise, but the patient is most likely to undergo a regression. As the tumor enlarges, displacing the brain of its limited space, the pain will become excruciating and the resultant death is very unpleasant, indeed. A very painful way to sign into the next life, if you believe in God, that is. May I go now?"

"Doctor, this is Special Agent Gibson, when you say regression, what exactly are you saying? That he'll become infantile on us?"

Without mentioning names and remaining strictly in the hypothetical, what I mean is that the patient will seek out a place of safety or where they believe they're safe. Listen, I have to go now. Anymore questions, you can call my attorney." The click told Rachael and Gibson a dial tone was soon to come, as the connection had been terminated.

"What did we just learn, Rachael?" Gibson said with a degree of frustration on his face. "Did we just hear that defense say our killer is legally insane and will never stand trial?"

"We don't try cases, Hollywood" she began, using his nickname for the first time. "We get them off the streets and let the attorneys worry about all the legal crap. Let me make another call, but I think I have the answer." She exclaimed, as she dialed another number.

"Bones, Rachael Hart," she said as someone answered the other end of the call. "I have a scenario for you and I need your help."

Rachael explained the medical and legal situation of Evan Felder, while Gibson listened admiringly. "So, when a patient or victim goes into this regression, what does that mean?"

After a long pause, the forensic psychiatrist said, "He will go back to where it all began, as if he might be safe or find a cure of some sort."

Where it all began, Bones?" she asked.

"That's my guess, yes. Anything else?"

"Doc, Gibson began, "under the circumstances Rachael described, do you think our guy is legally insane?"

"Well, without examining the patient, I can't give you my clinical opinion, but I would say that your guy is fifty-fifty. He has as much chance of being sane and he does insane" the psychiatrist answered.

"So, there's a good chance he'll never face trial. Is that what I hear?" Gibson asked.

"As much a chance as he goes facing trial. I said fifty-fifty."

"Thanks, Bones. I got to run. Just got the warrant on this guy and gotta find him before he hurts someone else. I owe you, Bones."

"Let's have lunch again and you can tell me all about your psychotic episodes" the shrink said, laughing aloud.

"I'd like that Bones; it's been a while since we've done that. I think the last time was on the case with the child killer, Johnny Lee Childress, Remember?" she asked.

"Yeah, the guy that claimed God saved him and gave him a new life. Right?"

"That is him. How about next week, we make it a date for lunch?"

"Same place as usual? The hot dog stand down the street or the place next door, Uncle Charlie's?" he asked her.

"You call, Bones, Gotta go though. I'll let you know when we have this guy and you can come to see him." She said.

"I'd love to, Rachael, before the quacks get their hands on him."

"You got it, Bones. I'll call you soon. Thanks." She said and hung up.

Gibson looked at her longingly. "What did we just learn, again?"

"I think I know where we're going to find our Mantis," Rachael began and stopped, "Well one of two places really."

"And? Care to enlighten this finely tuned federal agent of your clinical hypothesis?" Gibson mused.

"If you're going to be your old self and a smartass, no, you can figure it out yourself."

"OK, what's your theory, Sergeant? Where shall we dispatch our troops?" Gibson asked.

"Where it all began, Mr. FBI. Where it all began. Get it?"

"Where the tumor began? What the hell do you mean, Rachael? Inside his head?" Gibson replied in a frustrating tone.

"Either Rush Street, where he began this killing binge he's been on or Wheaton, where he was first told he was dying.

Gibson looked at her. "Where it all began, huh? Could he believe it all began with an event, you think?"

"Maybe, if he believes his problems began then. I can't see why he wouldn't, Rachael returned.

"Remember, I told you we interviewed people in Wheaton?" Gibson asked meekly now.

"Yeah, I remember when you did that to me. Why?"

"Quentin's father said that he thinks his son did something bad to another boy and wanted out of town before something happened to him."

"And? What do you think happened to whom?" she asked him

Well, as a finely tuned federal agent, I think Quentin did Felder. Either raped him or had him on his knees and got scared, like most bullies do."

"You believe Quentin took off because he raped our killer?" she enquired of him.

"That's why the Mantis targets homosexuals. He fears being one now or because he was raped by one." Gibson said as if some clinician.

"You men are animals. You'll stick those things anywhere. Disgusting." She said teasingly as she opened her folder.

"What's all that?"

"It's our Battle Plan," she answered, as she laid sheets out on the table.

"OK, Napoleon, what's your plan here? We are going to ride elephants into combat?" he asked.

"That wasn't Napoleon, you moron. That was another whack job, probably trained at Quantico."

"You sure it wasn't Napoleon?" Gibson asked as he rounded the table to see what she had laid out.

"Yea, it was Hannibal, as in 'Silence of the Lambs,'" remember?"

"Damn, the Bureau tried so hard to solve that case, along with who shot John Kennedy." He answered.

"So, here's my plan. We split into two groups."

"Ah, were two groups, Rachael," he interposed.

"That's not what I mean you rude bastard. Now listen, will you?"

As Rachael explained how she wanted a mixture of FBI and C.P.D. forces, with two SWAT teams to cover areas likely to find the Mantis hunting, Gibson understood how fortunate Daniel Salvino really was and admired him deeply.

Chapter 17

"Sergeant Hart?" the caller asked.

"Yes. Who is this and how did you get my number?" she enquired.

"Ah, dispatch gave me your number, Sergeant. This is Officer Meakins from the Traffic Division," the young, male voice exclaimed, as if she would recognize his name.

"And? I'm kind of busy here, Officer Meakins. Is there a reason you called?" she asked, then added, "What did you say your star number is?"

"I didn't Sergeant, but think I'm following the guy you call the Mantis."

"Well, then just pull him over and arrest him, Officer. You're about the tenth one so far that has spotted him," she returned sarcastically.

"Yes Ma'am, I could attempt that but there are a lot of people in the area and that could present a concern for their safety in case he runs."

"Where are you, Officer?" Rachael asked.

"Ah, Ma'am... I mean Sergeant; I'm here on Rush Street, by a club called 'Mothers.' Know where that is?" the young cop answered.

The location caught Rachael's attention. "Where it all began: raced through her mind. "What's he in, officer?"

"A green Jeep, Sergeant. Temporary plate from Wisconsin on the back," he returned.

"Officer Meakins, I am giving you a direct order to make no attempt to stop that vehicle or apprehend the driver. You are to follow that vehicle and report only to me. You understand that?" she shouted into her cell phone as she jogged out of the Homicide Division heading for the elevators, not even slowing to grab her jacket.

"Yes Ma'am, I mean Sergeant. You are heading towards me then?"

"I am 10-20 your location is about ten mikes, Meakins. You lose that man and I'll have you in the parking garage working lug nuts. You got me?" she said while riding in the elevator to the parking area where her squad was kept.

"AH, yes Ma'am. Parking garage. 10-4. I copy that. Will remain behind the Jeep until your arrival," he answered, but Rachael had already hung up.

Inside her emerald green squad, lights and siren at work, she called Ben Ori.

"Ben, it's him! The son of a bitch is on Rush Street right now. I'm in route, but we got a rookie cop that's following him and he could lose him," she said, as Ben could hear her siren blasting in the background.

"I'm about ten minutes out, code three, but I'm afraid Felder is going to lose him," she said, as Ben could hear her siren blasting in the background.

"If we put more units on him, he'll surely run or hurt someone. We can't risk that, Rachael." He replied.

"I know. I'm not sure I have a plan yet to take him down once I am there. The guy is in a crowded neighborhood and could do anything."

"I'll have units converge, but remain hidden on stand-by, just in case," Ben advised.

"Tell them to stay west of Rush and when I need them I'll call on Tac 2," she replied, referring to the Tactical frequency for special operations.

"Will do. You be careful, Rachael, this isn't some guy you want to challenge. He'll hurt people before he returns to hell or wherever he came from," Ben said fatherly now.

"I understand, Ben," Rachael said, as her squad was closing on the general area where Officer Meakins was located.

Killing her lights and siren now, so as not to spook Felder if he sees her, she contacted Meakins for his location and arranges an intercept point, so that she can assume command and effectuate the capture.

The thought never crossed her mind to contact her counterpart at the FBI. Gibson, as she had plenty of officers to capture Felder and deliver him to the Cook County Jail. Indeed, it is her case, she assures herself, as justification for not calling Gibson and bringing him up to speed.

As she nears the location, she advised Meakins to switch his radio frequency.

"Meakins, where the hell are you?" she shouted into the mic.

"I'm not exactly sure, Serge. I just transferred to this district and don't know the streets yet. I see some bars and a hotel," he said meekly.

"Meakins, Rush Street is full of bars. Where the hell are you at with cross-streets?"

"We're stopped right now, Serge. "I can't see any cross' street and this guy keeps looking over his shoulder at me," the young cop pleaded.

"Meakins, don't you spook this guy. Act like you are looking at everything but him. You got that?"

"Serge, I think he made me as a tail," the officer said frantically.

"What are you doing? Are you making eye contact with him?" Rachael asked a note of desperation in her voice. Do not make eye contact, Meakins. I don't want this guy hurting anyone."

"Serge, we're beginning to move. The light must have changed. I'll try to get you a cross-street and you can take over."

"Relax, Officer Meakins, we're not positive this is our guy. It probably isn't, but we'll check him out together. OK?" Rachael said, trying to calm the rookie, but she knew that the man in the green Jeep was the Mantis. She just knew it. Could feel it, but wouldn't tell Meakins as he was the lead officer on the fugitive's capture.

"He's turning, Serge. We're going left on...no, he just turned right from the left lane. What do I do, Serge?" the rookie shouted.

"Turn left, Meakins and then turn around and get your ass back on that Jeep. Any idea where you are yet?" Rachael asked excitedly.

"Hang on Serge, I'm trying to get back through the intersection and find this asshole," the young cop said, discarding federal regulations regarding cursing on public radio frequencies.

"Damn, I have a red light, Serge. I gotta shoot across the intersection."

"Do not use your lights, Meakins!" she shouted at her mic.

"Serge, I'm new, not stupid. Damn, that was close. A bus damn near took me out. Don't they respect cops here anymore?"

"Meakins, Rachael began with a laugh, "just find that Jeep and save the comedy for Jerry Springer, will you?"

"I see the Jeep ahead. It's not moving Serge." Her heart fell, as she pictured Felder on foot now and escaping their capture. "Talk to me, Meakins."

"Hang on, the Jeep is moving now. Looks like he was waiting for me, Serge. I think we have a problem here," he replied.

"He's playing with you, Meakins. Stay with him now, no matter what he does. He's made you, so there's no sense in acting. Just get me a cross-street damn it, now," she ordered.

"Wells, Serge. I just crossed Wells," the rookie said proudly.

"Got it! I'm a couple of minutes out. I'm bringing back-up with me, so you hang tight, Got that?"

Sure, Serge, but what do I do if he takes off on me?"

Rachael had the identical concern. If the Mantis fled, a high speed pursuit, at this time of day and in this popular area could be lethal to a number of innocent people." Let's see what he does, Meakins, but this is probably just practice.

"Serge, I don't want to screw this up," the young cop said as a simple statement.

"You're doing fine Meakins. Just remain calm and we'll get there. I'm closing in on Wells. Where are you now?"

"Serge, he just pulled to the curb. I'm in front of the Premier Hotel. Looks anything but premier. It looks like a whore house. Oops, sorry, Serge."

Ignoring the female slur, Rachael asked, "Is he out of the vehicle, Meakins?"

"Yes Ma'am, he just waved to me."

"Do not let that man walk away, Meakins. I'll be right there. What's he doing?" she asked with the excited tone of a hunter whose dogs have located a scent of a fox.

"I think he's waiting for me. I'm exiting, Serge. I'll be 10-29 at the Premier," he shouted into the mic.

"Meakins, do not approach this man. I repeat, do not approach this man. He is to be considered armed and dangerous. Got that?" Rachael said as she activated her emergency lights now. "Meakins? Meakins, you hear me?"

Silence.

Switching back to Tac 2 for the SWAT team and back-up units, she advised them to converge, Code Three on the Premier Hotel on Rush Street and switched back to the prior frequency.

"You copy? This is Officer Meakins to Sergeant Hart. Do you copy?"

"I've got you, Meakins. Where are you and where is the subject?" she said as calmly as she could.

"Serge, I need some help here. This guy is laughing at mead waiving. This old man is really out there, Serge."

"Just follow him, but keep a safe distance, Meakins. The cavalry is coming. You hear me? The SWAT team is minutes out, so just keep a visual on this guy," she replied.

"He's going into the whore...I mean hotel, Serge. Do I follow him?"

"You follow, but maintain a safe distance. Do not get into an elevator with this subject. You got that? No elevator. We'll shut the building down if we have to, but you stay out of his way."

"Copy that, Serge. I'll maintain a visual and report his movements." The rookie returned.

"I'll be right back Meakins," she said to the young cop and waited. "Meakins?"

"Yeah Serge. I'm here. The subject just flipped me the finger."

"I'll be right back, Meakins, she said and switched back to the SWAT frequency.

"this is Hart. Where the hell are you guys?"

"Serge, we're getting there as quickly as we can in this traffic."

"Go Code Three, as the subject has already made our uniform and is now on foot" she directed.

"Got that. Going Code Three," the SWAT commander returned.

"The subject is on foot now. Repeat, subject is on foot at the Premier Hotel on Rush."

"Be there in two mikes, Serge. Tell the uniform to hold the fort."

"10-4, I'll be there too, so look for me," she said.

"Will do. See you in..." Rachael never heard the rest of the transmission, as she switched back to Meakins.

"Meakins?"

"Here Serge. You're not going to believe this, but this guy just showed me a knife he has up his left sleeve. Damn thing looks a foot long. What do you want me to do?" the rookie returned.

"Meakins, do not approach this man, but if he makes any threatening move towards you or anyone else, you will shoot this bastard and let me worry about the paper work." She said matter-of-factly.

"Will do, Serge. I am drawing my weapon so the subject knows I'm serious."

"Meakins, do not engage this guy. That's what he wants here. You copy?" she asked him.

"Copy Serge, but the subject is entering the elevator in the lobby."

"Don't go in that elevator. Secure the area as best as you can. Copy?"

"Serge, he's gone."

"what do you mean he's gone, Meakins? Is he in the elevator?" she asked.

"No, Serge, he isn't. I waited in the lobby like you said and when he entered the elevator, I stood back to see what floor it stopped on. Then, the elevator door opens again. It never moved and the subject is done. Just like that," the rookie apologized.

"Meakins, the elevator has a front and rear door. He's going towards the rear exit. You copy?"

"Copy, Serge. I'm headed for the front desk to see where the rear exit is," the rookie replied.

"Shit!" Rachael shouted and saw the blue and white squad of Measkins.

"Meakins, I am on site now, I repeat, I am on-sight. Where are you?" Rachael shouted into her portable radio, exiting her squad and running to the front of the hotel.

As she raced into what was unquestionably a whorehouse, a couple who may have been negotiating a price for services, looked at Rachael. Glock in one hand and walkie-talkie in the other, and hostility went opposite directions.

"Meakins, where the hell are you?" Rachael asked.

With sirens approaching now, Rachael began to relax a little. "Serge, we're out back. This guy waited for me. He wants me to follow him," the rookie said, as if he were up to the challenge.

"Meakins, he's not waiting for you. He's waiting for me. It's a game with him. Stand down, officer. Stand down and observe. Copy that?"

"Serge, you'd better hurry up them" the rookie said in an anxious voice.

"What's happening?" she fried back at him.

"Serge, he's waiting for you on the steps going up to the elevated trains. What do you want me to do?"

"Meakins…" she began, as she contemplated ordering the young cop to approach Felder or shoot him to prevent his escape or wounding of others, but then knew they lacked sufficient justification to simply open fire on him.

"Serge?"

"I'm here! I'm coming out the back door now. Where are you?" she said.

"Break left, Serge. We're over here. See us?" the rookie said softly.

Not two hundred feet away, she could see Meakins, his weapon aimed skyward and there, at the top of the stairs stood an old man, his hair disheveled, clothes rumpled, with gnarled hands and eyes that reflected red.

Sprinting to join Meakins, she shouted into her radio.

"This is Hart. We're at the elevator platform. All units converge. Repeat, all units converge."

Walking up besides Meakins, her Glock trained on the silhouette above, she told Meakins to stand down.

"Evan Felder, I'm Sergeant Hart with Chicago P.D. and I need to talk to you. May I come up there?"

"I can hear you just fine, Rachael, "the Mantis replied, using her first name as if to catch her off guard. "I really need to talk to you, Mr. Felder. I don't think the world understands you. I'd like to understand you more," she said.

"You are as beautiful as they say, Rachael. The sweat that makes your shorts cling to you shows all those female curves. I see your nipples are hard. Is that for me?" he asked.

"Mr. Felder, It's over. I know all about the tumor and the pain. I'll help you" she replied, ignoring his sexual affront.

"Of course you will, Rachael. They'll kill me for what my Master had had me do in preparation for his arrival. That's your cure for me." Evan said as he watched her and kept looking to his left as he did so.

"Let's not hurt anyone else, Mr. Felder and I assure you that you will not be harmed either" she replied.

"There are people around me, Rachael. People are waiting for the train. Would you like to see them sacrificed to the Dark Lord?" Evan asked her.

Realizing the threat and not being sure of taking such a long shot with a handgun where she would wound Mantis and by the time she climbed the stairs, he could slash a number of people, she lowered her big Glock.

"Look, Mr. Felder, I'm putting this away and so is the officer next to me," she said aloud, but in no more than a whisper, she said to Meakins, "Where the hell is SWAT when you need them?"

"Rachael, you've played the game well, but you are no match for the Dark Lord. I have to go now. If you follow me, these people's lives will be on your hands," Evan hissed.

"Mr. Felder, your family needs you," she said as she attempted to distract him. In a whisper, she told Meakins to find out what trains were due in shortly.

"Ah, you met my lovely wife then." Evan said in a theatrical tenor. "You should have seen her when we got married."

"You have a family Mr. Felder. Is this how you want to be remembered? Is this how you want your kids to remember you?"

"They will all understand when my Master arrives and I save them from damnation, Rachael. I may even save you," Evan said and smiled.

Rachael could see his orange-ish teeth now and his eyes were a fire mist color. "Mr. Felder, can I take the place of those people up there?"

"Rachael, you are as brave and courageous as you are beautiful, but these people will keep me from the rifle shots, huh?" he replied.

"I've ordered everyone to stand down Mr. Felder. Do you see any weapons pointed at you?" she pleaded.

"Do not fear the arrival of my Master, Rachael. Welcome him and I will tell him you are a warrior and worthy of his service." Evan said and disappeared from sight.

"Dam it," she shouted. "This is Hart, I want units at every damn stop the train makes. I don't want this guy walking away from us. I'll be following," she said into her radio before running towards her squad.

"Meakins, wait here and see if this guy comes down those stairs. If he does, shoot him until your weapon is empty. You got that?"

"Got it Serge. Thanks."

Not wanting to discuss the rookie's emotions or why he wanted to thank her, she sprinted off to her squad. As she got there, Ben was just arriving.

"Ben, will you get this Jeep towed to our forensics people? Felder was driving it," she said as she jumped into her squad and tore off.

Watching Rachael's lights shrink in the distance as he sped to keep up with the southbound commuter, Ben said to himself. "Sure, Sergeant. I'll take custody of the subject vehicle and arrange for its secure transport to our techs," he said to no one. Anything else I can do for you?"

A cavalcade of cars, trucks and vans, all with those flashing blue strobes punishing the night, looked more like a Hollywood scene, than the morbid hunt for a man no longer fit to live in this world. "Get this son of a bitch, Rachael," Ben said. "Shoot him if he tries to touch you."

"Do we have a transit cop on that train?" Rachael asked the dispatch officer who was coordinating the chase.

"Sergeant, those are random assignments and they don't have assigned runs. They float from train to train. We have no way of knowing unless we get the transit people on the line and that'll take too long," the voice said.

"Then get someone in plain clothes on this train at the next stop," she commanded.

"We already have a narcotics officer waiting on the next platform, Serge."

"I'll be on the platform too," Rachael said and laid the mic on the seat next to her, so she could focus on driving.

When the commuter cars came to a screeching halt, there were officers all over the platform and they rushed to the open doors. One by one, each car was examined for the presence of Evan Felder the Mantis.

"He's not on the train, Serge," the final word came.

Rachael had seen the Mantis step onto the train and then it struck her. The double door, where Felder enters one set and walks out the opposite side, which meant that Meakins and Ben, along with a few other officers might still have him cornered.

"Ben, Felder may still be on the platform there," she said eagerly into her cell phone.

Ben looked around and saw about a dozen C.P.D. officers milling about. "You people, get up there on that platform and look at every support underneath it.   He might still be there someplace," he shouted.

"Meakins, Ben, he's a rookie." Rachael said.

"Gotta go, Rachael. I'll call you if he's still here." Ben said as he closed his phone and brought his radio up. "Meakins, you still there?"

"Yes sir, at the bottom of the steps."

"Our subject may not have gotten on the train, but is on the platform on the other side of the tracks. Be alert, Meakins. We have units coming to you and or the other side." Ben said, wondering about how their subject could get off the platform. Then it struck him. "All units, the subject is on the tracks someplace. I want you to focus on any area without a platform and steps."

"Mr. Invincible, you're on those tracks where the third rail can help you discover your destiny, aren't you?" Ben said to no one.

At that moment, a solitary figure made its way towards a bus stop, having gotten on a commuter car and exited the rear door, dropping down to the tracks and stepped from cross-tie to cross-tie, mindful of the third rail that carried thousands of volts which powered the huge electric motors on the commuter. Felder.

Chapter 18

"Ben, it's my fault we missed him there." Rachael said.

"Nonsense! You couldn't charge up those steps and risk innocent people, so you did exactly what you did," Ben responded. After Evan Felder managed to escape capture, Rachael had alerted every form of public transportation, as the Jeep he operated was in the forensics lab being meticulously disassembled.

"He's right, Rachael," Gibson chimed in, after arriving on the scene when FBI scanners picked up the transmissions and advised him.

"We've saturated the area and he doesn't have his own transportation now. He'll turn up," Ben added.

"I don't like standing around and waiting for this psycho to give us another body," she replied.

"Then, I have an idea, Rachael. Let's you and I go to a few of these fine hotels around here, flash his picture and see what we turn up?" Gibson suggested.

"You think he's familiar with this area and that's how he managed to slip out?" She asked in return.

"Stands to reason, actually. He is from Wheaton and worked downtown. How else did he become so familiar with this area?"

Ben watched the exchanges between the FBI agent and his second-in- command, recalling those by gone days when he was in the streets, instead of pushing paper. "I think I'll get some paperwork done, if you too will excuse me," Ben said as he walked back to his car. Neither of them commented on his departure, instead, plotting hotels they each would investigate.

"Do you feds have access to our Tac Two frequency?" she asked Gibson.

"Rachael, how do you think I was notified of your show here tonight?" he replied.

"Figures. OK, I'll be on Two," she said as she turned and walked towards her squad without waiting or any answer from him.

For the next hours, Gibson and Rachael went from hotel to hotel, or in most instances, flophouse to flophouse, questioning the questionable staff who routinely violated the record keeping laws, as hookers brought John after John to their fine establishments for entertainment and servicing.

"Nice city you have here, Sergeant Hart. Seems like you have more whorehouses than any other city I've been to," Gibson said taking a break.

"It wouldn't surprise me to learn that you would have the experience to make such a determination, Mr. FBI." Rachael returned, as she parked her squad in front of one seedier establishment. "I'll get back to you. I have another five-star hotel to visit."

"10-4, I'll be 10-99," Gibson said smiling, which simply meant that he acknowledged receipt of her last transmission and was taking a bathroom break.

"Have you seen this man?" she asked the man behind the counter.

"You a cop, lady?"

Opening her jacket, where her Glock and star were both attached to her belt, she said, "This man?"

"Man, you're in the wrong business. You could make ten times what they pay you with the city."

Tired and frustrated, she leaned closer to the clerk so her point was made. "I'm going to have about fifty cops here and we're going to go from room to room. Am I clear here, pimp?"

Realizing the magnifications of such a visit, the clerk looked at the photo. "Yeah, he's one of ours. Why do you want him? Are you Vice or Narcotics?" He asked her non-chalantly.

"What do you mean he's one of yours? Is he here now?" she asked eagerly.

"Just went back out. Paid me another day's rent and walked out with his suitcase."

"Gibson," she shouted into her radio. "I found his home base, get the hell over here," she said, and then switching to another frequency said, "All units converge on my 10-20, Code Three."

"Ah Christ. You gotta bring the troops in here like a Springer episode?" the clerk asked.

"What room?" she said bluntly.

"Second floor, third door on the left." The clerk said.

"Key" she commanded while holding out her hand.

The clerk was well aware of his obligation to protect the sanctity of his guests' rooms. However, given that the guests here were committing felonies for sexual pleasures, he really had no desire to incur the wrath of the police.

"You reached over and took this key, lady. I didn't give it to you." The clerk monotone, as he handed her the bare key.

"Don't worry about record keeping, pervert. Worry about what I may find in there," she said as she drew the Glock and began climbing the stairs.

Neither the key nor the doors were numbered. "Nice place you have here Mr. Felder. Perfect for your line of work," she muttered as she slid her back along the grungy wall, stepping quietly towards the door indicated by the clerk.

When she reached the third door on the left side, she carefully slid the key into the knob and turned ever so slowly. Click.

Opening the door with her foot the light from the hallway illuminated the interior of the tiny room and she could see that no one was inside.

"All units, subject left my location on foot, carrying a suite case. I want the buses and trains covered from my location," she shouted into her radio.

"Are you sure I can't talk you into joining the FBI?" Gibson said as he strolled up to her.

"Not a chance. And miss all this>" she said as she extended her arms.

"Nice hotel. This four or five stars from Triple A?"

"You probably keep a room here, don't you?" she asked.

"Nah, too expensive. I have a tent down by the rail-yard," Gibson returned as he entered the room flipped the light on with a pen and began looking around.

"I can see why he's so upset," Rachael began. "Someone was sleeping in his bed when he wasn't in it."

"You got uniforms that can seal this off. Let's see if we can find where he walked off to, shall we?" Gibson asked her.

Outside the flophouse, having uniform cops seal off the entire floor, Ben was waiting for them.

"So, you two found the Mantis's lair," he began, "A thousand to one shot and you two unearth it," Ben said as Gibson and Rachael approached.

"I thought you were going to do paperwork, Ben. What brings you here?" Gibson asked.

"I can't risk leaving you two alone in the community that I serve and protect," he returned.

"He came here, packed a suit case and walked out, just like that," Rachael said.

"And what are you doing to find him?" Ben asked Rachael.

"We have saturation, Ben. We have units at the cab companies, alerted the Transit Division and monitoring all traffic stops, in case he has another vehicle around here."

"Sounds like you have everything covered. "Ben said, as he turned his giant frame towards Gibson. "And you, Mr. FBI, what are you doing for us?"

"Uh, I haven't activated our forces because this is your case and we don't want to offend your Department." Gibson replied.

"Nice line of shit, for saying the FBI isn't doing shit right now. That about sum it up?"

"Lieutenant Ori, I am the liaison agent between C.P.D. and the FBI. You haven't asked us to do anything yet." Gibson said coyly.

"Well, just as well, I guess. Saves me from tripping over fibbies all over the place," Ben mused.

"Sergeant Hart?" a voice on her radio asked. Picking up her radio and pushing the talk button, she replied. "This is Hart."

"Serge, this is Meakins."

"I copy that, what can I do for you? We're kinda busy right now. If you need a performance letter for your boss, come by tomorrow and I'll write a nice letter for you."

"That's nice, thank you, but that's not why I'm contacting you," Meakins returned.

"Then what can I do for you? Do you have the subject in custody?" She joked.

"No, Ma'am, but I can. He's standing across the street from me," the rookie said back.

"What? Where are you, Meakins?" Rachael asked him.

"I'm at the train platform, Serge. I returned here because criminals always return to the scene of the crime, don't they?"

"Meakins, we're on our way there. Do not lose this guy." Rachael demanded.

"That's not a problem, Serge. I already know where he's headed," the young cop said.

"How's that, Meakins?"

"He's on the express line to O'Hare airport."

Gibson asked her what significance there was to that answer from Meakins.

"There are no stops between there and the airport. We either get him there or on the other end," she responded.

"I think I better alert my people," Gibson said as he withdrew his cell phone and walked away.

"We're going to get this guy, Ben" she said in earnest.

"I know you will. Just don't get too close to him. This guy is different somehow." He replied.

"Gotta go. I'll stay on Tac Two, in case you need me," she advised him and ran off to her car.

After both of them were gone, Ben said to himself. "Seems all I'm good for is the damn paperwork," then went upstairs to wait for forensics to appear and take over the "scene log," where everyone has to sign before gaining access to the area.

"Gibson you on this channel?" Rachael asked blindly.

A few seconds later, she was rewarded with, "Right here Rachael."

"Stand down. Tell your people to stand down. I know where the subject is headed," she stated.

"What do you mean, stand down? We're here to help you, not steal your thunder," Gibson replied.

"We can't risk him hurting anyone. He's heading to where it all began, Gibson, she said back as if he should solve the riddle instantly.

"What the hell are you talking about?"

"You don't get it, do you? He's headed to where it all began."

"You sure you don't need a refresher at Quantico? He's headed to Wheaton, where this all began years ago."

"And you know this how?" he asked now.

"It's where he feels safe, Mr. FBI. Now, stand down and tell your people to observe only and do not attempt to intercept him. We can't risk anything happening to people on the commuter or at the airport."

"I hope you're right, Rachael." Gibson said sincerely.

"So do I, Hollywood. So do I," she answered.

As she propelled herself down the streets towards Meakins, she recalled Ben's words "Don't get too close to him."

"All units," Rachael said into the mic calmly. "This is Sergeant Hart of Homicide. No action is to be taken with this subject. Observe and report. I repeat, no attempt to arrest subject. Follow and report back to me."

"They're right, you crazy bastard. You're heading back to where it all began and I'll be there waiting for you." Rachael said as she entered the expressway heading west towards the city of Wheaton.

Chapter 19

"Wheaton," was all Evan snarled as he flung the cab door open and tossed his suitcase on the rear seat, before sliding in.

"That's expensive, buddy. You got that kinda cash? I ain't going all..." was as far as he got before Evan dropped five, one-hundred dollar bills over the divider.

"I like Wheaton, mister. Nice town or city. Is there something I should know about? You being chased or something?" the cabbie asked.

"Drive. All you need to know is how to count. You can count, right?" Evan replied, which came out as if in slow-motion and deep, as if he were in some auditorium.

"Sure, I can count. If this runs out, I suppose you got more. This real money?" the cabbie shot back. While the cabbie examined the bills with his inside light, where he noticed each bill had the Treasury heliograms authenticating them, he happened to look in his rear view mirror and saw Evan.

His face is pale. Very pale and lined a hundred times that of Einstein's worst photo. He could see Evan's nostrils flare out with each exhalation, and then contract again, as air was sucked into his lungs. And his eyes did not resemble eyes at all, but burning embers from a fire.

"You all-right? You don't look so good. Want me to take you to a hospital or something?" the cabbie asked.

"Do you believe in Heaven?" Evan hissed.

"Yeah. Doesn't everybody?"

"Then you believe there's a Hell," Evan said as he lifted his hideous right hand with arthritis badly twisting and deforming his joints, that his hand resembled a claw, more than a hand.

"Arthritis, huh?" the cabbie began. "Damn shame. That must hurt like hell sometimes."

"Wheaton," Evan said, emitting a foul wind from his mouth as he did so.

"Whew!" the cabbie replied, turned towards the front and swung the Yellow Cab into main stream traffic in front of the airport terminal. He kept the inside light on, fearing being alone in the dark with his highly unusual fare, which made identifying Evan and following the cab a walk in the park.

"He's in a cab, Rachael" Gibson began. "Stay with me and we'll see if you're right."

"I am," she returned. In the background, she could hear Gibson on his radio now. "All units stand down. We are to follow only. Until we are capable of taking this guy safely, we do nothing."

"I've got about a dozen people here Rachael and our Hostage Response Team is in route to Wheaton. Any particular place you want them?" he asked.

"Tell them to hold outside of town, but I think our boy is headed for the high school," she replied.

"Where it all began for Evan" she returned. "Is he headed west?"

"Yep. Where will he turn? Remember, I don't know your area yet."

"He'll end up on 59, which runs directly into Wheaton. Let me know if he deviates."

"Rachael, you going to have kids?" he asked her.

"What? Have you lost it, Hollywood? Before action, you think about your pecker?"

"I wish I would have had a family, "he said, ignoring her diatribe. "Khoren is pretty lucky. He has a wife and kids who moved here because I did some John Wayne shit in Miami," he said.

"You OK, Gibson?"

"Sure, I just think about what my life would have been like, had I met a girl that could tame me and we had kids." He replied, and then continued. "I wouldn't be here tonight, as I wouldn't have buried that damn quarterback's precious toy into the home of a politically connected asshole."

"You were in pursuit of a murderer, as I understand and he is currently residing on death row, so I'd say you did a great job," Rachael retuned.

"I told Khoren we were headed for the museum section, Rachael," he said. "I lied to him because there is something unusual about this asshole and until we have him in custody or I'm standing over his dead body, I don't want him around."

"You think Khoren can't handle it anymore? Is that what I'm hearing here?" she asked.

"Not at all, Rachael. Khoren is more of a handful than you think. He just never talks about it. I just don't want him around this time, in case I screw this up and they want to transfer me again. He and his family can stay here and have a home."

"You're not going to screw this up. We'll take this guy down when he can't hurt anyone else. We just can't take chances," she replied. "This guy is no demon or hellion, Gibson."

The pause told her that he was weighing his options. Then he replied. "Don't let him get close to you Rachael. If he does, empty that cannon you carry into his dark ass. You got that?"

"You're the second person that has mentioned that to me. What's up with that? You and Ben talk behind my back?" she asked.

"No, Miss Smarty. I don't talk to your boss behind your back," he said and then another pause. "This guy is different, Rachael. I don't want to see you take any chances with him. Our BAU people can't wait until they can dissect him.

"Our people are looking forward to meeting with him, too. I'm sure it'll be years before he finally faces a jury, but that's not our concern. We do our job and let the attorneys worry about all that."

"We're turning here, hang on." Gibson said.

"You should be exiting and heading south about a quarter mile to Highway 59, then west again," she said.

"Yeah, I see a sign with 59 and staying in the right lane. Looks like he's coming to you Rachael."

"Hang on, Rachael, I got a call coming in from my boss," he stated, before switching the call. When he came back on the line he said, "Well, seems both of our bosses are joining us in Wheaton."

"What? Ben's coming out there? I haven't heard him on the radio," she replied.

"He's in the car with my boss. I guess they want to watch us at work."

"I don't like them being friendly. We hate fibbies." She exclaimed.

"Well, seems like you and I are the catalyst for change, Rachael. We're proof that the FBI can work with the locals and solve cases." Gibson returned, a grin replacing the consternation. "Where are you and your people positioned?"

"We're in a parking lot, behind a hot dog stand so he won't see us. Where're your people?" She asked.

"They're in a fire department lot. They told the firemen they're on a secret assignment and not to let the Wheaton P.D. know they were there."

"Are they on our Tac Two frequency?"

"Yep. They'll move when you give the signal, Boss," Gibson mused.

"Let's see if he comes directly to me. Where it all began, Gibson," she replied.

"You never answered the question, Rachael. You plan to have kids?"

After a long pause, she replied. "First, I have to convince Daniel that an Irish girl is the woman of his dreams. Irish girls aren't into the 'baby daddy' reference, but Dad or father, as in marriage."

"Need me to flash my badge on him and have a little man-to-man talk" Gibson joked.

Daniel isn't impressed with badges and guns. He's more into swords and knives."

"That leaves me out. I cut myself damn near every time I slice tomatoes. Guess you'll have to tame him on your own."

"Daniel and I are in love, but we have such different lifestyles. He needs to stop jetting all over the world, or I have to quit the Department and become arm candy for him   See what I mean?" she asked, wondering why she was being so open with him that way.

"Well, good luck to both of you, Rachael. You're a hell of a cop." Gibson said, and then added,   "But you'd wash out of Quantico. The physical training would be too much for you."

"You fibbies are so conceited. See why we hate you guys?" she joked.

"We're stopping, Rachael. Looks like we're at the high school," he said as he dodged driving past Evan in the cab.

"We're rolling here. Once he's in the school, he can't hurt anybody else and we have him contained" she replied.

"Hold it, we're moving again," he said quietly.

"Where are you heading now?"

"Not sure, but I think we're going towards his home. Maybe he needs to see his family?"

"Oh shit! She exclaimed. "We can't let him go in that house. He could do anything in there."

"He's not going to hurt his own kids. Rachael. He might be saying good-bye," he returned.

"Your call, Gibson. You're the man out front." She said.

"Stand down, Rachael. Let's see where this takes us. He needs to do something." Gibson explained, as he resumed following the cab.

Chapter 20

"Oh my God," his wife said. The agony she felt at seeing the demonic changes the tumor had brought on Evan was apparent. He had aged a hundred years at least, she thought. "Don't you come inside, Evan, I can't let the kids see you like this."

In a raspy voice, slow and deep, Evan said, "I know, I just came to give you this" he hissed at her.

"Oh Evan, why did God do this to you?" she said as she laid her head on his shoulder and wept openly. "God," he began and took a labored breath, "had nothing to do with me. I serve a different Master, my dear." Evan said, as he set the suite case down on the porch and with a hand that resembled more like a garden trowel, he pushed her hair back.

As she smelled his fetid breath and body odor the stench of his rumpled clothes, she swore to herself that she would never worship Christ again. Not after he had needlessly punished her husband in this way.

Looking at his shirt, not daring to look at her husband in the eyes, she said, "Are you...?" She couldn't bring herself to say the word "dying," but each knew the question.

"Soon, my dear, soon," Evan said with that hisss, which his wife attributed to mounting cranial pressure, not an impediment imposed by the Dark Lord." I brought you this," he said, nudging the suite case with the toe of his night shoe.

"I don't know what that is Evan, but I'd rather have you back with me," she exclaimed.

"Tell the kids I love them and not to judge me harshly. We all serve our masters."

"The cops were here Evan. The FBI," she said pleadingly.

"I know. A man named Gibson," he returned.

"Evan, he and his partner, a woman, asked me about your dreams," she replied in almost a whisper.

"That was Rachael, my dear. She's a cop, not FBI," he replied bluntly.

"Evan, what do they want with you?"

"All of you will understand shortly, my dear. He is coming."

"Who is coming, Evan?"

"The Dark Lord. You'll see," he said as he turned back towards the cab. I have to go now, my dear. He calls me."

With that, Evan turned and shuffled, more than walked, towards the cab, leaving the battered suite case at her feet.

Once he was back inside the cab he said, "Go around... "Then inhaled with a rattling gasp, "the block," he ended with an exhale of foul breath.

"Jesus, buddy, you smell like death itself. You want I find a hospital?" the cabbie asked.

"Unless you would like to meet..." inhale, "your God tonight..." exhale "then you do as I tell you or my Master"... inhale "will have your balls for lunch," exhale.

The cabbie looked at Evan and would later swear to police that a wisp of smoke had come from his nostrils. "Around the block. You got it."

"We have been followed," inhale "since the airport." Exhale "yet you did not tell me," Evan hissed.

"Must have been the light and focusing on doing my job," the cabbie said nervously.

"You will not get," inhale a tip like that" exhale, as Evan tried to laugh.

"I don't need a tip, mister. I don't want any problems either. Whatever reason why those people are following us is none of my business."

"It's Gibson, but there's no Rachael. Inhale. Hold. Exhale. "I can't feel her." Evan hissed.

"Where to?" the cabbie asked in his best theatrical fashion, trying hard not to show his fear.

"Turn off…" inhale "your lights", exhale.

"What? I won't be able to see? That ain't safe; pal, just to lose them back there."

"Would you,…" inhale, "like to meet my Master" exhale "or go home to your family?"

Without hesitation now, the cabbie turned off every light and the cab disappeared into the night.

"Rachael," Gibson said frantically, "the cab just disappeared."

"What?" she shouted into her cell phone.

Chapter 21

"Do not"…"inhale, "use your breaks, "exhale. "Use the parking brake and stop here" Evan hissed.

Following the orders to a tee, the cabbie brought the cab to a complete stop in the middle of the road, in total darkness.

"Very good…" inhale, "you may go home to your family now…" exhale. "And you may keep the change," inhale, Evan said, trying his best to make a joke.

"Look, buddy," the cabbie began. "I think you should let me take you to a hospital. Whattya say?"

In the dark, the cabbie could see the glow of Evan's eyes, like two rubies, illuminated from behind.

"You are a good man, Mr. Kuman, I will speak to my Master on your behalf." Evan managed to say without the interruption of labored breathing.

"How'd you know my name?" the cabbie asked.

"This night is unholy, Michael…" inhale, "you should be at home with…" exhale "your family," he hissed. "Now go," Evan said as he exited the cab.

Without turning his lights on until he was a block away, the cabbie sped off into the night. By the time he reached the expressway and headed back to Chicago, he had already notified his dispatcher that he was signing off for the night and headed home with the flu.

With the moon obscured by a dense layer of cumulus-nimbus clouds, there was a little light, save for the orange glow of the street lamps. As Evan shuffled off into the night, the street lights went dark, one by one as he approached.

"I'm coming, Master," Evan managed to utter before there was no more oxygen in his lungs.

While Evan wandered the darkness, Gibson called the Yellow Cab company and after identifying himself along with a promise of immigration officers descending on the company if the dispatcher declined to help, he advised as to how Evan had exited the cab in total darkness and the cabbie had no idea where he was at that time.

"Rachael," Gibson began after dialing her cell phone again. "This fucking guy is a spook. The cabbie related how he had dropped him off in the dark and how his master is coming. I think he's really lost it."

"That would be assuming that he was sane at some point when he began all this killing. He's going to come to me, Gibson, she said flatly.

"I know, to where it all began," she exclaimed in an exasperated tone.

"Whatever he's doing, he's coming to me. The high school is here it all began and it will end. For some reason, he wants to die there, where he was violated by the bully.

"I hope you're right, Rachael. "Gibson said. "right now, we're got a psychopath in the dark, in a family type neighborhood and some secret god coming to see him. We're fucked."

"Come back to where we are and we'll figure out how to get inside the high school without alerting the locals and scaring him off."

"I have an idea, Rachael."

"No Hollywood, shit Gibson. I mean it! This is my goddamn case and I want you to get your ass over here with the rest of us. You got that?" she hollered into her phone.

But the phone was dead, as she had not heard him disconnect. "Goddamn you, Gibson!" she screamed as she tossed the phone on the seat of her squad.

Turning to the anxious faces of the C.P.D. officers awaiting her orders, she said, "OK, people, suit up. We have an undercover agent from the FBI here, so I don't want any accidents. We roll in ten, unless we hear from him before hand."

"I hear you father," Evan howled. "Please stop the pain," he whimpered while trudging along the pitch dark, as if connected to a wire.

When Evan reached the home where Quentin grew up and lived with his parents, he silently crossed the weedy yard, headed for what once was a lush garden of wild flowers. "I am her Master," he snarled in an almost inaudible voice.

Dropping to his knees, Evan began clawing at the ground, the long, brittle fingernails snapping at the first attempt to trowel the hardscrabble earth.

My name is Quentin," he repeated softly as he continued to scratch at the dry patch.

For almost a half hour, his hands gnarled and bloody, he kept digging like a dog from hell itself. Little by little, his hands managed to pull clumps of earth from the singular hole. All the time, he apologized to his Lord for failure.

Chapter 22

"All right, boys and girls "Gibson began as he addressed the FBI Hostage Response Team that awaited him at the fire station.

Firefighters watched in awe, as the black clad men and women, began genderless combatants, as vests, masks and helmets were systematically assembled and affixed to their bodies after years of training and experience.

Donning his own gear as he spoke, Gibson went on to advise his soldiers with, "This guy is absolutely, fucking cuckoo.   His mind has fried itself in bacon grease. He is extremely deadly and in the final stages of psychosis."

Gibson noticed the looks he was receiving from his troops and continued, "Yes, crazier than me," which drew a round of chuckles.

"You may think of me as a member of "Psychos-R-Us," but I have no idea why these whackos do this shit, but our BAU people live for it."

Calvin Gillings, the boss of the Chicago office of the FBI, watched Gibson from the sideline. While he had to admit Gibson possessed an unique oratory skill, it seemed to have the desired calming effect on the HRT members.

While Gibson continued his briefing in the background and readying himself for combat, if the Mantis so desired, Gillings and Ben Ori had their own thoughts about the situation.

"What do you think of him, Ben?" Calvin asked.

After a pause, collecting his thoughts, he replied with, "He's different, Calvin.   He certainly has a way of entertaining these people. Is that why you call him Hollywood?"

That question caused Gillings to snicker.   "Not exactly, Ben, Without going into details, let me say that some of his arrests have been high profile and expensive for the Bureau, even with millions of dollars seized from drug people each year.

"That bad?" Ben asked.

"Ever seen the movie 'Hancock' with Will Smith as some super-hero?" Calvin asked in return.

"Yeah, I did see that. He always managed to destroy something, even though he captured the bad guys, right?"

"That's the movie. Well, imagine my agent over there in tights and the ability to fly."

"Hmm, I think I'll leave that vision alone. I can't go home to Mom, with fantasies in my head about men in Spandex." Ben answered.

"He's a damn fine agent, Ben. One of the best I've ever seen. His dedication is unmistakable. It's just he risks himself, Ben. He has no fear or has no concept of dying in his vernacular."

"As you know, I have one of these fearless people too and I worry about her every time she goes into a situation like this," Ben replied.

"You see, as administrators Ben, we're supposed to displace ourselves emotionally, but I have never mastered that skill. I'm afraid for every one of my people there," Calvin said fatherly.

"Rachael's with our SWAT team and suited up as we speak. I don't know if man made weapons will work on this guy, Calvin."

The SAC looked up at him at this revelation. "Ben, do you believe this guy's Satan too?"

"What I am saying, is that there is something very unusual about this guy. You have to admit that" Ben intoned.

"I'll give you that he is the most unusual killer the Bureau has ever encountered, but I can't agree that Satan protects him or that he is the Devil incarnate. He's flesh and blood, just like us, Ben," the SAC said.

"Calvin, I've been a homicide cop forever. I've never seen anything like this Mantis character. He seems to have some evil machination to him, which is beyond the mass growing inside his head." Ben answered. Back.

"Our BAU people tell me that this tumor can make him think he's an angel or a demon but eventually he'll go down in a pool of his own blood."

"I have a feeling, Calvin that the pool of blood will be from bullets, not a hemorrhage. I just don't want to see any of our people's blood mixed in with his." Ben replied.

"Amen there," Calvin said and the two leaders began to laugh at the Christian gesture.

"Under no circumstances do you let this guy touch you or get near you," Gibson said to the HRT members. I don't want anyone getting hurt, unless of course, it's this Mantis character who believes he's the Devil."

"You know, Ben," Calvin started looking up at the Homicide Chief, "when I received the call from the SAC in Miami telling me that I had just inherited the FBI's most costly and flamboyant agent, I asked myself why I was being saddled with him," Calvin said as he inhaled deeply and gazed around the fire station. "Since he came to Chicago though, he has proven himself to be one of my best people."

"I detect something missing in your tone, Calvin," Ben said.

"Up until tonight, he has not been in physical situations and on his first one, he's the lead agent."

"And you're concerned he'll screw up?" Ben asked.

"Not exactly," Calvin began, "well there's that too, but I'm worried about him. He has no fear, Ben. He will sacrifice all, in the name of the Bureau or them with him."

"I think you might be under-estimating the members of your team, Calvin. I see every one of your people out there suiting up, as having the same dedication you speak of with Gibson."

"Don't get me wrong, Ben. I know every one of those agents will sacrifice, but Gibson will go the extra mile to apprehend this guy," The SAC returned.

"I have a sergeant just like that," Ben said.

Gibson, the H&K, MP-5 automatic rifle resting on his hip, reminded Ben of scenes from "Platoon," one of his favorite movies. "We are arresting a serial killer, people, not the Easter Bunny. If anyone gets hurt, let's let it be him. Let's roll," Gibson said as he headed for the black vans that would carry them to the fight.

"I think you and I are in the way here, Ben. Care for some hot coffee?" Calvin asked.

"I need to check on my people too then, I think we become observers after that. We see if the baby birds can fly or will fall to the ground." Ben returned.

"My sentiments exactly, but we still worry about our baby birds, don't we?"

"Whoever harms one of my birds will answer to me," Ben returned.

"Somehow, I think that you would harm someone who hurt one of yours. Especially, a certain red head," the SAC said with a huge smile on his face.

"That obvious, huh?"

"Damn right. Let's go see how she's doing."

Chapter 23

The dirt between Evan's knees reeked of an unholy scent, as if some unfortunate creature had recently been buried there and was in the early stages of putrefaction. As Evan dug deeper and deeper, the earth giving way much easier now and he was able to scoop large handful of soil now, the fetid odor intensified.

"I am here my lord. I am here," he repeated over and over, as if that was the motor that drove him onward, as if he were nothing more than a drone.

In a whimpering voice, Evan leaned over the hole he managed to open and said, "I have come for you Lord. I'm here" and carefully slid both hands, fingers extended, into the earth.

"We are together again, Master," Evan said, his eyes emitting a pale red glow now, illuminating the hole in the total darkness.

When Evan withdrew his hands from the earth, they cradled a bleached white skull, whose jaw had either fallen off or was claimed by years of being entombed in raw earth.

"Master," Evan hissed now, "as you have ordained, I have come for you. Together, we will show the world the powers of the Dark Lord."

Raising the mutant skull towards the blackened sky, Evan released an unholy howl, as if a choir of demons rejoiced in their Savior's return.

Lights began to pop on in the homes surrounding Evan and the grave he had opened, where he had hastily buried Quentin after clubbing him to death outside the bar that night before Quentin was due to report to the Army. For decades, he replayed the events of that night, again and again in his head. A hundred thousand times, he had relived that night, the crunch of Quentin's skull when he made contact with the maple bat after that vicious swing. A hundred thousand times, he apologized to the dead boy who had sodomized him, yet he did not deserve to forfeit his own life as a result.

A hundred thousand times. Evan regretted what he had done and had never been caught for, yet answering to a higher power now.

"My Lord, let us open the portal to our kingdom and behold the Mantis, grace to those who declare themselves to our service." Evan said, cradling the skull in both hands raised over his head, as if it were a chalice at some religious service.

"Behold people. The Dark Lord has cometh," Evan said loudly, as he meandered down the middle of the darkened street where one-by-one, the street lights went black.

Chapter 24

While law enforcement moved closer to capturing Evan, CNN decided to broadcast a "special report" on the man called Mantis. A tribute to the psychologically devastating implications the gruesome murders sustained on the average American, or as one anchorman put it, "A testimonial to a true sociopath."

"Good evening everyone," the first of two anchors, a man and a woman, "we bring you the remarkable story of a simple man, who, for medical reasons, became the number one murderer in America "the man said.

"Yes, remarkable indeed, as the man now identified as the Mantis, is no super-criminal, but an insurance executive, with no criminal record whatsoever." The woman said, while giving the camera her best Barbie doll smile and displaying politically correct cleavage for the male viewers.

We take you to the beginning, not where our law enforcement community wants us to avoid," he said.

"At this station, we uncover the truth and give it to you straight, not what we're told to say by any law enforcement or political entity," she exclaimed.

"Evan Felder and his family live in the modest community of Wheaton, as seen here from our surveillance cameras, where he commuted to Chicago every day to work in this building," the anchorwoman said, as a photo of the entry doors to the building which houses Evan's corporate offices were located.

"Our reporters have uncovered shocking news, that this Mantis, now being hunted by every law enforcement agency in America as a rabid killer, actually suffers from an inoperable tumor and resultant psychosis. In an exclusive interview, Mrs. Felder is seen pleading for her husband's life" the male counter –part stated.

Cameras panned from the family home in Wheaton, making the background a total blur, then halting on the face of Mrs. Evan Felder, as the lettering beneath the frame related.

"Mrs. Felder," the unseen reporter begins, "you've heard the horrible stories from law enforcement about your husband. Is there anything you want our viewers to know?"

Changing to a close-up, Evan 's wife dressed in simple clothing and manifesting the average working class Mom, despite receiving a quarter-million dollars from Evan and his agreement with CNN, she looks directly into the lens. "My husband is dying from a tumor that continues to grow inside his head and making his life unbearable. Evan is no psychotic killer. He's a father and has worked all his life to support his family. Until this thing began growing inside his head, he was just your average man." She said.

"Is there any message you have for law enforcement, Mrs. Felder?" the unseen reported asked.

With tear's flowing from her eyes, the camera brought in for maximum close up, she said, "Please don't kill my husband. He's dying and in pain, he's not some dog gone wild."

"In extensive discussions with our medical experts here at the station," the anchorwoman back in the studio began, "they relate a very disheartening story and the anguished journey towards death, patients suffer in instances like this."

Obviously beamed from the home of one of the network's hired guns, the anchorwoman asked the physician with a name too complex to spell out, so the station simply called him "Dr. K." The anchorwoman asked for his medical opinion.

"Thank you for having me on your show" Dr. K. began. "In an unfortunate scenario like this, the patient will undergo many painful changes, as this tumor at the center of his brain expands. The pain will be intense and chronic, requiring pain management, which usually results in narcotics. Very strong narcotics actually derived from opium or heroin."

"Dr. K." the Barbie asked, "will the patient likely suffer dementia or a psychosis as this inoperable thing continues to grow?"

"Oh yes," the foreigner answered, "the pain will be so intense that he will eventually go insane, especially, if he is not receiving pain management."

"Do you have a message for law enforcement, Dr. K?"

"Yes, I would like to relate something to them," he said, as the camera moved in for a close-up. "Please employ non-lethal methods to capture an obviously very ill and terminal patient. We can at least permit him a modicum of relief during his waning days on earth."

"Our sources," the anchorman now took control "deep within the law enforcement world, tell us that at this very moment, a large force of agents and officers are in the hunt for Evan Felder," he said sternly. "Let's go to our expert on police tactics and weaponry, we will have in our studio, a retired FBI agent and security advisor to international figures, Ron Barrett."

With the cameras pulled back now, revealing the presence of Barrett, sitting to the right of the anchorman at the desk, the anchorman asked, "Ron, in your experience, when law enforcement are in the hunt for a wanted murderer, what can we expect to see?"

Ron Barrett's previously broken nose, which may never have been set by a physician, is the retired FBI man's visible legacy for years of dedicated service.

"Well, then the FBI is closing in on a subject wanted for murder, like Mr. Felder is, their primary concerns are for the safety of the community, then the safety of the agents and lastly, the safety of the subject," he said, using his fingers to represent his points, as he related them.

"And what kind of weapons will they carry, Ron?", the Barbie doll asked, as if they were drinking buddies from a local tavern.

"Well, the FBI has expert armorers," he began, while looking at the anchorwoman. "In other words, it has some very sophisticated hardware in its arsenal for just about any scenario one would encounter in the field."

"Would the arsenal include explosives, for example?" she asked.

"Without question." He said sternly. "The HRT, or Hostage Response Team, will have full panoply of weapons, including plastic explosives."

"When would explosives be employed?   I mean, "the anchorwoman started," would the FBI detonate explosives in capturing Mr. Felder?"

"I cannot say for sure what their plans are, but in certain circumstances, the FBI will exert explosive force which is likely to kill the subject."

"Is there some special authority needed from a higher-up, like Washington perhaps, before explosives can be deployed?" Barbie asked.

"No, that call is reserved for the lead agent, as the decision would likely need to be made quickly and on the spot."

"Thank you, Mr. Barrett, for joining us tonight in our studios," the Barbie said in closing.

"Thank you for having me," the expert said just before the camera resumed the close-up of Barbie and her counter-part.

"We have just received an email from the parents of one of the victims attributed to the Mantis," the anchorman said urgently. While holding a piece of paper he appeared to read along. "While we mourn the loss of our son, we now know the medical circumstances that motivated Mr. Felder. We've been told that Mr. Felder is the cold-blooded killer called the Mantis, but we were never informed of Mr. Felder's medical condition. It is our sincere wish that Mr. Felder is treated with all respect and dignity that may be afforded a person with his conditions. After all, he is a human being and obviously not responsible for his actions.

"Why would law enforcement keep such critical information from the medial and families of the alleged victims?" Barbie asked.

"According to the insiders in the law enforcement world, the release of such information is beyond protocol and policy. In other words, they simply arrest people and leave the courts to sort things out." He replied.

"Sort of like automations or robots?" Barbie returned.

"Emotionless is a better descriptive. Emotionless."

The camera focused just on Barbie now, obviously the person who would close the broadcast." And there you have the revealing truth behind the hunt for Evan Felder, who is referred to by the law enforcement as the Mantis. What they didn't want you to know is that Evan Felder is dying and probably not responsible for his actions. All we can hope for now is the humane capture and treatment of this family man, who is stricken with horrible medical circumstances. Even the families of the victims; plead for his safety and medical treatment."

Back to both anchors now, the male anchor said, "We return you to regularly scheduled programming at this time. For all of us here at TV 7, we extend our hopes and prayers to the families who lost loved ones and to law enforcement agents for a safe and humane arrest of Evan Felder, so that he can be treated for his medical conditions."

"Good –night everyone," Barbie said, as the logo and network music took control of the screen.

Chapter 25

"You're not going to believe this," Ben began, after calling Rachael on her cell phone," but Calvin Gillings and I are watching your Mantis right now."

"What? Where?" Rachael asked excitedly.

"Well, Calvin and I went for coffee after watching the FBI people suiting up. I insisted on coming there to see how our people are doing and while driving through the neighborhood, we drive right upon your subject. Or, at least we believe it's your guy."

"What the hell does that mean, Ben? Are you watching Felder or not?" she asked of her boss.

"Well, Calvin and I both agree that it must be him, but he's different Rachael," Ben replied.

"Don't start that crap too, Ben. IS he hovering above the ground or something? Maybe lighting his way by raising an index finder like ET?" she said sarcastically.

"Not exactly Rachael," Ben said guardedly. "What do you think Calvin," Ben asked in the car.

From the background, Rachael could hear the FBI agent's voice. "I think it's our guy. The skull kind of gives it away."

"What?" Rachael returned. "What skull is he talking about, Ben?"

"It looks like our Mantis here, dug up an old friend someplace, Rachael," Ben answered.

"Are you two drinking?" she asked.

With a chuckle, Ben said to Calvin, "I told you she'd think we were drunk. You owe me."

"Ben, you're serious about this?" Rachael asked.

"Quite. The Mantis, at least the one we're following right now and doesn't give a damn that he's the center of our headlights, has a skull tucked under his left arm, cradled like a baby. He appears to be talking to the skull. Listen." Ben replied.

Very faintly, Rachael could hear a voice in the background of Ben's call. "We're coming Lord."

"You hear that Rachael?" Ben asked.

"Yes. What are you planning to do, Ben? Are you going to arrest him?"

"We, as in Calvin and I, are not going to risk this neighborhood. We're going to follow the subject and when he is clear of homes and families, you people can take him down. He's headed for some place in particular, so there's no rush."

"Ben, he's headed for the high school. That's where it all began." She responded.

"Then he'll be easier to arrest there and we don't risk public safety." Ben exclaimed.

"Ben, I just received a call from the office. Seems that our staff, has plenty of time to watch TV."

"And, what was on that I need to know about?" Ben asked her.

"Seems that TV Station 7 did a special, on our guy here. They portrayed him as a victim of the tumor and that he's not legally responsible for his actions," she replied.

"Well, that was nice of them. And I suppose they even had some of their so-called experts testifying that the Mantis is insane?"

According to the detective that called me, one of the victim's family has asked us to pamper him until God calls for him," Rachael answered.

"It sells thier program, Rachael, whether they believe their own crap or not. It sells. So, don't get all upset about it" Ben consoled her."

"Ben, they made us sound like murderers, not the sonofabitch you're following."

"He's turning the corner, Rachael," Ben said, as he ignored her concerns about the Department.

"You want us to roll, Ben?"

"Hold tight. We can't risk lives here. He's not going anywhere on foot."

"Have you notified Gibson?" she asked.

"Calvin is on the phone with him right now. He's not moving yet, either. Until we can contain this guy, we don't want anything spooking him."

"10-4, we hold for your signal," Rachael said in a disappointed manner.

"Hang on there, sergeant, you are going to get to cuff this guy. We can't risk any lives out here though." Ben responded.

The silence was deafening, as Ben held the phone to his ear anticipating a sharp retort from Rachael. "I think we're coming up to a park or something. Stand-by, but load up and get ready to roll," he told her.

"We are loaded up, Ben. And very ready. Do you have a location for us?" she enquired.

"Seems like we're in a school zone, Rachael. This must be your high school." Ben replied.

"It is on the west side of the street, according to the compass in the fed car. It's two stories high and sits about a hundred yards off the street I'm on. Has a big parking lot directly in front," he said.

"Ben, you described about half of the office buildings around here. I suppose you want to point out the flagpole too?"

"Well, there is one of those, too. It's dark out here Rachael. If we turn the spots on, we can worry the locals. Your Mantis is heading right for it."

"Ben, is there an old building across the street with huge columns our front, like a Southern home?"

"As a matter of fact, there is. Are we at your high school?" Ben asked her.

"Yep, What's Felder doing, Ben?"

"He's aging and shuffling slowly towards the front of the school. Appears he intends to go inside and then he's all yours." Ben told her.

In the background Rachael could hear Gillings on his phone, presumably to Gibson. "Roll. It's the high school. Silently though!"

"Ben?" she asked him now.

"Roll, Rachael. Come in silent, no lights. Let's see if we can take this guy quietly, shall we?"

"Rolling," she returned.

"Well, I guess we both watch the future of our agencies at work, Calvin," Ben said after handing up.

"I guess so. We could try arresting this guy, Ben?"

"Neither of us is wearing a vest and all we have is side arms," Ben replied.

"My vest is in the trunk and I have a couple rifles back there. Want to try this?"

"There is something about this guy that tells me it is not going to be an easy arrest, Calvin. Besides, we can't steal the thunder. It wouldn't be right."

"So, we just watch this guy try to break into a public building, a felony, and wait for subordinates to effectuate the arrest?" Calvin asked Ben.

"That about sums up my plan, yeah." Ben replied with a grin. "In our reports, we observed the subject and contained him in a large building, which turned out to be a school, until support officers moved in to make the arrest safely," Ben responded.

"He's approaching the front door, Ben

As Evan walked or shuffled is the most appropriate term now, still cradling the skull in the crook of his left arm like a running back in football, the light from the front of the building fully illuminated him.

"Is that Felder, Ben? Jesus, look at him," Calvin said as he looked out the windshield of the squad car.

"You see what I mean now, Calvin? There's something very wrong here."

"His back is humped over," the FBI chief exclaimed.

As the two veterans of the law enforcement watched, Evan stopped at the front door and turned to look at them.

"You might need Jesus tonight, Calvin. Look at his guy!"

Under the white lights at the front of the school, they could see him clearly.

Evan waited for his two pursuers to get a good look at him, before he turned back to the glass door, stuck his right hand through the glass and stepped into the dark interior of the school.

Ben said to himself, more than his federal counterpart, "Where it all began, Rachael. Don't let him touch you."

Calvin Gillings, the highest ranking FBI agent in the City of Chicago, simply made the sign of the cross.

Chapter 26

The travertine walls of the old school, carried an echo like the Swiss Alps and as the two pursuers sat quietly in the car, they could hear him consult with the evil powers that drive him.

"We are here my lord," Evan bemoaned. To the skull that rested in his left arm, he said, "Master, we have come home. Our lord is near."

"Rachael, the subject is inside the school. Approach with extreme caution. Repeat, approach with extreme caution." Ben said into his phone.

"10-4. we're about a minute out. Advice feds we'll take the back of the school." Rachael told him.

"Calvin's handling that now. "Ben answered then continued "Rachael, this guy is… really out there. Be very careful with this."

"I got you Papa." Rachael joked.

"Gibson," Rachael could hear in the background. "You will approach from the front. C. P. D. had the rear, so hold your fire until you have a positive subject. We don't want any of our people hurt here from friendly fire."

"Calvin, I'll go around the back, just in case this fox tries to run out the back door," Ben said as he slid out of the car and drew his revolver.

"Got silver bullets in that thing, Ben?"

"That's for were wolves Calvin. I think we need holy water for this guy." Ben said just before turning and walking towards the building.

The sarcophagus-like silence from the granite flooring to the travertine walls, gave the school an unholy touch. Outside the rear doors, Ben could no longer hear the wailing pleas from within, but he could sense the presence of something beyond mortal.

As if on a wire, Evan trudged down one darkened hall way to another. "We are here my lord. I am sorry that I have failed thee. Please take this pain away Lord, as I am your servant. I did not know, my Lord," Evan said as he shuffled one foot in front of the other.

Calvin slipped through the door frame which once held glass, his Smith & Wesson automatic held before him in both hands. Immediately he became invisible in the pitch black interior. Placing his back to one of the cool walls, he listened and awaited the arrival of the HRT team.

As the flashlights pierced the shroud of darkness inside the school, signaling the arrival of his HRT, Calvin felt more than heard, the baleful cry from deep within the bowels of the school.

Gibson was the first to see him and approached. "Is he still in here?"

"Yes, yes he is, but there is something at work here that puts us all at risk Calvin replied.

" Are you all-right?" Gibson asked him.

"Don't let his guy get close to you."

Chapter 27

"Rachael, are you there?" she heard in her headset.

"Gibson, we're at the rear door and about to enter. Where are your people, over," she said.

"Just inside the front door, preparing to search and locate subject. Do you have any idea where he's heading here?"

"Where it all began, Gibson, over"

"We can hear him. Can you? Listen." Gibson replied, refusing to say "over" like in the movies.

"I thought that was you moaning" she quipped.

"Do you believe in the Bible?"

"I'm Irish, Gibson and let's keep this discussion professional, shall we. Everyone is on this channel." responded.

After a brief pause, where she heard the wailing of some wounded animal as it echoed down the halls, Gibson said. "Then you'd better ask God to watch over you tonight."

"We're entering the rear now. Make sure everyone is alert here. I don't want any accidental shootings here."

"My people wish likewise, Rachael. We're heading down the corridor." He said.

Rejoining Calvin in front of the school. Ben confers with the FBI chief.

"Calvin, we don't have real authority here in Wheaton, but you do. I think we're dealing with something more than...what we usually face."

"I was thinking the same thing, Ben. When that bastard entered this place, he looked like he was a hundred years old."

"I've never seen red eyes, except in movies. This one worries me, Calvin," Ben stated.

The look the FBI Chief returned was confirmation enough for Ben. Once inside Gillings' squad car, he radioed Wheaton P.D. and directed them to secure a one-block radius, which meant no traffic whatsoever and for local officers to awaken every family and have them evacuate their homes. The later, would be under the pretext of "a gas leak at the school," which meant starting with the homes closet to the school, first.

Switching back to Tac Two, Calvin contacted Gibson. "Be advised that locals will be evacuating the area. Listen up everyone, Lt. Ori and I agree that extreme caution is to be exercised here. Under no circumstances are risks to be taken. Do not let the subject get near you."

"What exactly are you expecting from us?" Gibson asked, unsure of how to take someone into custody without getting near them.

"Our subject has undergone some changes. He's old and weathered, despite his age. Something is at work inside him and he is capable of anything. That's what I'm saying." Calvin replied, not wanting to sound as if insane himself if he advised the teams that he believed most, if not all, of then would not survive the night.

"Roger that, chief," Gibson said. "Ok, let's find this guy and get home and have a beer."

The flashlights, which are mounted under the barrel of their automatic rifles, danced from side to side as if angry fireflies battling each other, as the agents and officers began their incursion into the depths of the school. As beams of light hit objects around them illuminating old locker doors, scarred and scratched from swinging Master locks, to old wooden doors on the classrooms, step by step, brought the teams closer to the demonic howling somewhere within.

"OK, everyone, listen up!" Ben began, "the school is shaped like an 'H', according to overhead images we have here. Gibson, you are Team One and you have entered the bottom left leg. Rachael, you are Team Two and you have entered the upper right arm. When each team reaches the intersection with the common hallway, you will not split your teams. You will each post two people at the intersection, sweep the remaining side of the 'H' and then return to the common hallway. We don't have blueprints, so we can't be of more help to you. Everyone copy?"

"10-4," Rachael returned.

"Copy," Gibson sent back.

"Ben," Rachael began, "is there a way to turn the lights on in here?"

"We have no clue how to do that. Aren't there any lights in there? Nothing?"

"It's total black here. I've tried light switches, but nothing comes on." She replied.

"Go to night vision, everyone. I repeat, go green." Ben ordered.

This is the latest technology in thermal imaging, or night vision that indicates minute temperature differentials. Then translating into active images for the person wearing the devices, generally appears in green, with higher temperatures being the deepest green. Everything has a temperature signature, be it a door, puddle of water or human being, the variances in heat equate to a greenish image to the wearer of night vision equipment or through scopes.

"Going green," Rachael stated.

"Likewise" Gibson added

The exchange of concerned glances between the two veterans and the respective chiefs, said all that was needed to be said. Both leaders were quite concerned for the safety of their people.

Being green or "under the hood," as it's sometimes called, beams of light resemble light sabers from the Star Wars movies. If a beam is reflected back into the night vision "eye," it can temporarily blind the wearer. With that knowledge at hand, the beams no longer bounced carelessly, but more controlled and substantially lower, allowing the night vision equipment to perform.

"Where do you think he is, Rachael?" Gibson asked.

"The Boys locker room, where he was raped by Quentin," she replied.

"Where it all began," he intoned.

"Where Quentin enslaved him by violating him."

After a pause, "So he's calling Quentin now? Is that the wailing?" Gibson asked, as he lead Team One from room to room, clearing each as they went, along with opening every locker without an internal padlock, in case Evan was hiding inside.

It was when both teams heard multiple voices that their incursion halted.

"Rachael, I don't think our guy's alone," Gibson said.

"Sounds like two or three others. Proceed with caution," was all she said. As she and Team Two methodically searched room after room, locker after locker and any other space where a man could hide, she wondered if a psychotic person was capable of uttering different voices to match the multiple personalities inside them.

As both teams converged on the common hallway to the 'Design, the members all noticed that there was a discernible thrum, as if huge machinery were nearby and that is was getting warm. Within a hundred feet, the inside temperature had risen ten degrees or more, reducing the effectiveness of the night vision equipment along the way.

"We're holding at the opposite end. There will be no firing of any weapons from this vantage point. I repeat, no firing of weapons. Friendlies are on both ends." "Copy that. Hold fast," Rachael returned. "Losing green here," she said as she removed her night vision headset.

"Do you have a visual on anything Rachael?" he asked her.

"I have a double door with a pinkish glow coming from and around the door frame." With her flashlight, she read the placard on the door. "Boys locker room" Gibson. I'm standing right here.

"Losing green will be right there," Gibson returned.

Within seconds, Teams One and Two merged into a single force, before the badly faced doors that said "Boy's Locker Room" misspelling "Boys" with the use of an apostrophe and making it the possessive form.

"You and your team secure the area. I'm going in first," Gibson directed.

"And why is that?" she asked.

"It's a boy's locker room, Rachael. There might be naked boys in there," he said smiling.

"You are so full of shit," she returned and pulled one of the doors open. "You coming?" she asked.

Realizing that getting her to remain in safe haven territory, Gibson said, "You go left, we go right" and the teams parted, entering the locker room.

The heat intensified, well over ninety degrees now and the team members resisting loosening or removal of their heavy garb.

"Damn, where's this heat coming from?" Rachael asked.

No one replied, as each had their own thoughts on the genesis for the intense rise in heat.

"Anyone have thoughts on this reddish glow? " Gibson asked.

"Yeah, we're walking into hell" a male voice replied.

"Any family man can go back," Gibson said, then added, or family woman" for political correctness.

Once each team made its way through locker after locker inspections, again to insure that the Mantis was not inside and attempting to avoid capture, the two teams met at another pair of double doors. This pair, unlike the first set was swinging doors and said "showers" on the plackard.

Standing before this last set of doors, both teams realized that the wailing had ceased and that thrum of machinery assumed control.

"Whew, it's hot in here. No wonder our taxes are so high. They've got the thermostats turned all the way up," she said while trying to inject a bit of levity into the hunt for the Mantis.

"I'll go first, Rachael. You follow," Gibson said in a chivalrous tone.

Rachael began to protest, but the look in Gibson's eyes asked her not to. "On three?" she asked.

"Sure. Three," he said and rolled through the double doors in a summersault.

The maneuver caught Rachael a bit off-guard, but the reasoning was not lost on her. If an armed subject were waiting to shoot officers breaching a room where they were hiding, their weapons would most likely be trained chest-high. By vaulting in to the room, Gibson gained speed, surprised the plane-leveling advantage of requiring Evan to re-aim any weapon he might have.

As Rachael rolled into the ceramic tiled room, she saw Gibson, poised against a wall and motioning her to join him. "Team leader, hold your positions. I repeat, hold your positions. Do not breach this area." Gibson ordered.

The thrum was almost deafening in the cloistered shower. The tile seemed to insulate or intensify the sound, while emitting heat from the individual tiles.

"Don't touch the walls," Gibson advised her.

"The tiles are glowing" she remarked.

"There's your tax dollars again," he joked this time.

"You see him?"

"Yeah, he's just around the corner. Got a mirror on you?"

Mirrors are a tactical tool to see around corners and avoiding being shot by subjects who wish to keep their freedom, at your expense.

When Rachael produced her mirror, Gibson told her to take a look.

Easing her mirror past the walls end, she obtained a view of Evan, inch by inch, until she could risk no more and expose her hand.

Seated in the corner, the tiles around him a bright red, as if capable of searing meat, sat the lone figure they had been hunting. Or, was it? All that looked even remotely familiar was the face, yet it was so lines with layers of wrinkled flesh, even that resemblance was questionable.

Evan sat cross-legged, cradling the skull with missing jaw, in his left arm. His hands were claws now, the fingers more like tines of a trowel than workable digits. The fingernails were hooked like talons and a thick, orange colored material. His hair was long and wispy, although easily discernible as being a pasty white.

What captivated Rachael's attention, however, was none of the attributes above, but the Mantis's eyes, which were no longer eyes as humans know them, but burning orbs, like the hottest coals in the bottom of a campfire.

"Ah, Rachael Hart" a booming voice said, but not coming from Evan's pursed lips. "You are even more beautiful in person."

Quickly withdrawing the mirror, she looked at Gibson, as if he might have an explanation for the apparition around the corner.

"You and Melvin flatter me," the voice said. "You are very brave in coming here," as if holographic or without origin.

"Evan." Gibson said, "FBI. Can I talk with you?"

"That weakling failed me Melvin." The booming voice returned.

"I know he's there. I can see him" Gibson countered.

"He ceased being a man when he let me stick my cock in him and made him bleed," the voice said with a hint of laughter.

"Then you won't mind if I talk to him," Gibson returned, while taking Rachael's mirror and sliding it out to see Evan.

"Ah, you want to see us, Melvin, yet you are too afraid to step into view. Are you going to use Rachael for that, Mr. FBI?"

Manipulating the mirror up and down to get a more brooder picture of Evan and his hiding place, he saw no weapons in Felder's hands.

"Seen enough, Mr. FBI? Behold, the Mantis, Melvin." The voice announced. "I am the Mantis, Melvin. Come and get me," the voice taunted.

"Evan, I don't want anyone hurt here. I want to help you," Gibson replied.

"Help Evan, Mr. FBI? Evan was a coward. He hit me from behind with a bat," the voice stated.

"Is this Quentin?" Gibson asked.

"You have always been dealing with me, Mr. FBI. Evan could never have done what I have. I am the emissary for the Dark Lord, Melvin not that Bitch whose ass I enjoyed right on this vary spot."

"I'm stepping out Quentin. I just want to talk. OK?" Gibson asked, while Rachael looked at him as if he had lost his mind.

Holding the mirror, Gibson stood, keeping the reflection of Evan mid-frame.

Erasing his face around the corner, he could see Evan, seated in the corner. The ceramic walls directly behind him a bright red from intense heat, yet his tattered clothes were neither smoldering nor burning, despite direct contact.

"I thought you wanted to speak to me, Melvin? Why are you hiding like a coward" the voice taunted him, yet Evan's lips did not move.

"Yes," Gibson said weakly. "Yes, I do want to talk with you. I'm stepping out, Evan" Gibson said, and then corrected himself. "I mean Quentin."

With Rachael pulling on his arm in protest, Gibson took a step into plain view, his hands slightly raised to show he was not armed.

"Rachael is afraid Gibson. Are you?" the voice asked as Evan lifted his head to look at him.

Without showing emotion, or at least hoping that he had not given his revulsion away. Gibson looked at the remaining life form of Evan Felder. His back is hunched like Quasimodo in the bell tower, long white hair and the weathered face one sees of seamen who exposed their flesh to sun and salt, day after day, year after year. His hands, that no longer resembling the opposing digits of a human, but more like claws or clubs with talons. The eyes, however, captivated Gibson's focus, as they seemed more like portals to a well-stoked furnace, no longer capable of vision. And the skull with the missing jaw-bone, resting on the crook of his arm.

After recovering from the initial shock of Evan's form, Gibson noticed two thin wires that he traced skyward, where a six inch pipe, with white letters saying "gas" traversed the length of the shower. Draped over the gas line was a dingy white elastic belt, like those waist trimmers hawked by celebrities on television, affixed to the belt, startled Gibson.

"What's that for, Quentin?" Gibson asked.

Showering the bared ends he held mere inches apart, Evan mumbled. "The Master said I am safe this way, that you would not risk everyone."

"Evan? I need to talk to you Evan," Gibson said.

"Evan is my bitch, Melvin. Anything I want to poke that ass, he'll bend over." The voice said.

"All units, we have a bomb here. I want everyone to clear this building immediately." Gibson directed. Looking over his right shoulder, he looked directly at Rachael and said "Everyone. It's just he and I now," not sure if he should say Quentin or Evan.

"Gibson" Calvin's voice came over the headset." I want you out of that fucking building right now. All of you move."

"Your boss is a smart man, Melvin. I can feel his presence. Benedict Ori is here as well. My. I am flattered. I have the FBI and the Chicago Homicide here. The Mantis is pretty important, isn't he?" the voice intoned.

"Go, Rachael," Gibson said to her, shrugging off her hand. "Get out of here damn it," he shouted at her.

A feminine tear escaped the corner of her right eye, as she turned and walked out.

"OK, Quentin, It's just you and I now. What is it that you want?" Gibson said bravely. "You want your pal Sergio Medrano from CNN for another of your manifestos? Maybe some time with David Letterman?"

"Clever Melvin. Comical almost, but I want nothing from you or your superiors," the voice fired back.

Holding a hand close to the glowing ceramic tile as if to warm it, he could feel the heat build as his hand grew nearer.

"Cleaver trick, Quentin. How'd you manage this?" Gibson asked.

"The Dark Lord is coming, Gibson, Soon," the voice replied.

"I thought you were the master, Quentin?"

The hearty laugh that came forth startled Gibson at first. "Melvin, I am but a servant, but master to the pitiful form before you. My Lord is coming and will take Evan with him."

"I need Evan here, Quentin." Gibson stated.

"Gibson, get out of there now. The Bomb Squad is a few minutes out. Everyone is clear. Get out now and that's a direct order," Gilling' voice came over the headset.

"Your boss is afraid, Melvin"

Gibson looked at Evan and said "My boss doesn't understand. We're just talking here, right?"

"Do you believe in God, Melvin?" the voice said in a monotone.

"I believe in all things, Quentin: Gibson replied, never taking his eyes off of the bared ends of the two wires that would detonate the belt.

"Are you prepared to face Him, Melvin: Is there fear in your heart?" the voice asked in a strong, powerful boon like a jet breaking the sound barrier.

Outside, well past the parking lot for safety purposes in the event the gas line was blown apart, Rachael could hear the conversations inside. In fact, everyone could hear and the apprehension was readily apparent, as hands twisted and faces were contorted by the grimaces of fear.

"Gibson" Rachael said softly," get out of there," she managed to say as the earth began to quake.

The explosion, if one could call it that in a report was more akin to a volcanic eruption, a magnitude never recorded as such.

As glass, brick and splintered wood was hurled omnidirectional, the ground beneath the school appeared to split at first, the catapulting huge portions of the building skyward.

Flames belched from the torn earth and the parking lot buckled like a giant wave was passing underneath, sending squad cars twisting and turning in to the night sky. Those team members unfortunate enough to be there, screamed in agony as their flesh was seared like raw meat on a blazing fire.

As Rachael lay prone on the grass, she could see the epicenter of the explosion, which claimed the entire building simultaneously, the beams that made the roof and the roof itself, burst into the shards of flaming debris, as a brilliant red light was emitted, threatening to ignite the darkened sky.

A crevice formed around the foundation of the school, allowing smoke and fire to escape. Then, with a mighty roar, the school was lifted and dropped back into place, where the remaining remnants of walls and steel supports, crumpled inward.

Everyone who survived the holocaust swore they heard voices, screaming and anguished, while refusing to believe they heard the dying soul of a fallen brother.

A brilliant red light encompassed the school from the crevice and in an instant, the school was no more.

As night returned, all that remained of the school was molten steel and charred brick that lay in a smoldering heap. Not a single object was a flame.

One by one, the team members stood and helped comrades to their feet. No one spoke, but surveyed the devastation in disbelief. A brother had been lost and even the eyes of veterans were moist in remembrance.

"You all-right, Rachael?" Ben asked from behind her.

Turning towards him, she nodded and gently laid her head on his heaving chest.

Chapter 28

Throughout the night, the team members huddled near the SWAT van, silently recounting what they had seen and heard. Some renewed their faith to God, while others cursed him for allowing a dark force to claim a brother.

Fire trucks pumped water on the smoldering remains, while troubleshooters for the gas company tested the area for escaping gas and ruptured lines.

Ambulances carted off the wounded, mostly suffering from superficial burns, their combat gear protecting them from the brunt of the force and flames.

Wheaton P.D. called in all of its active and reserve officers, to cordon off the area from the curious, the media and the macabre. A "meals on wheels" truck appeared and complimentary coffee and bottled water was given to everyone.

Calvin and Ben leaned against the federal squad, sipping hot coffee and answering questions from their respective superiors. It was all part of their job descriptions, but when they looked at the members of their respective teams; each agreed that they resembled survivors of some earthquake or catastrophic event, than combat ready veterans. Although locals and feds resent each other, these two teams melded into a singular society of mourners.

A news crew filmed the entire event as if it were the sequel to the mindless attack on the twin towers in 2001. Ben actually purchased a copy of the show, which had scenes in black and white , as if dated before Kodacolor, along with close ups of grieving faces without jurisdictional boundaries. The wounded were shown bandaged or being loaded into the backs of waiting ambulances on gurneys, giving the overall scenario a war-like patina, as though these modern day warriors were fortunate to have survived.

In reality, of course, they had survived the inferno that engulfed the high school, because of the bravery of one man who believed his life was forfeitable, because he had no family or children who would miss him.

When the school's remains had cooled and the firefighters began the unenviable task of searching the twisted scraps looking for human remains, the images were nothing short of heroic. When the head of the FBI Crime lab was interviewed by one Sergio Medrano of the Associated Press, Mr. Whitehurst, an explosives expert who was trained in the military tactics, stated that the peculiar aspect of this particular detonation is there was no "debris field."

When an object is subjected to an explosive force from within, such as a firecracker for example, the external portions are blown outward or upwards, depending on the shape or location of the charge or charges. An "uncontrolled" blast, such as that from natural gas or even a fragmentation grenade, explodes in a spherical pattern, or "uncontrolled." When spectators gather to watch the demolition of a major building, what they are really seeing are a vast number of "controlled' detonations on support columns and generally in a computer orchestrated, sequential manner and the building collapses inward, on itself.

While Whitehurst guided cameras around the perimeter of the school, he pointed out visible signs of a horrendous explosion for the interior of the school, as steel supports were bent skyward like arthritic fingers reaching from a fiery grave. Once the cameras had sufficiently captured those images for viewers to comprehend,

Whitehurst stood on the outward edge of the crevice that rent the earth and faced away from the school's remains.

"Now, take heed, people. Look around the perimeter of this building and you will not find a single brick or piece of roofing, beyond this spot."

At that, the cameras panned the area to authenticate that expert's conclusion. While squad cars were found on their sides and scorched, as tribute to the explosive theory from Whitehurst, the area was devoid of any building materials whatsoever.

"What you see here is an anomaly. While we have an explosion, with a concussive force sufficient to toss squad cars about like toys, along with fire and flash sufficient to burn the officers and agents here, there is no debris field. What rests behind me is more akin to an implosion, than explosion."

"And how do you explain this Mr. Whitehurst?" Medrano asked.

I've been around explosives all my adult life and seen just about every crime scene from Waco, Texas to the twin towers and there is no human explanation for what you witness here. It's as if a giant vacuum sucked the concussion into the ground." Whitehurst concluded.

"And what was the source of this particular explosion, Mr. Whitehurst?" Medrano asked.

"I listened to recordings of communications and I heard the missing FBI agent describe a rudimentary pipe bomb that the suspect affixed to a large natural gas pipe inside the school." Whitehurst said guardedly, as he knew the question to follow.

"Could that have been the genesis for this explosion, sir?" the Associated Press station chief asked.

Troubled by the question, Whitehurst said, "Let me be perfectly clear here. I only have preliminary facts and conclusions to work with, as our Crime Lab people will dissect this place, a pipe bomb, affixed to a major feed line for natural gas, could destroy a building such as thi8s and the ignition of natural gas in the supply line, would cause an eruption in the earth along the course of the line."

"Is that what occurred here, Mr. Whitehurst?" the veteran interviewer asked.

A blast of this magnitude could not be the sole result of a pipe bomb. Therefore, this blast required a secondary and far more deadly genesis. Natural gas is a viable source for such destruction, but natural gas detonations are not controlled and we would have a major debris field here and the secondary explosion inside the gas supply line would be linear, where the ignition followed the gas line, not the oval shaped crevice we see here." Whitehurst said in a circular explanation that disagreed with itself.

"Thank you, Mr. Whitehurst, you've been very helpful," Sergio said before the lights on the cameras went out.

"So, Mr. Whitehurst, what the hell happened here?" Medrano asked as his arms were extended towards the rubble in the background.

"Honestly? No quoting me? I haven't a damn clue. It defies every physics rule for equal and opposite reactions. We should have bricks and shit from that school over a quarter-mile radius, yet not one piece is beyond that crevice."

"Any hypothesis Mr. Whitehurst?" the cameraman asked.

"Were you a veteran, son?" Whitehurst asked.

"No sir, I went to college, not war" the young man replied proudly.

"Well, some of us had to die for you to have that choice, but I don't hold that against you, "the FBI expert began. "Let me ask you this then. Are you religious?"

"Yes, sir. Lutheran, actually. Why?"

"Combat veterans know that God exits, as everyone I know had prayers they would repeat before, during and after a firefight with enemy forces. What I see here and again, I will deny ever saying it if held to task, is that God and Satan had a little duel here last night. As far as we know, we have one FBI agent missing, along with a wanted fugitive he was arresting. No one was killed outside this hole in the ground, despite a dense concentration of law enforcement personnel right where we're standing. Explain that, if God wasn't here to protect them and the families in this neighborhood?" he challenged.

"Then why couldn't God save your agent?" Medrano interjected.

"You forget, Mr. Medrano, Satan is a powerful entity and throughout Biblical times, God has never been able to destroy Satan, who is also referred to as the Dark Lord in Black Mass services and such. They are opposing forces with seemingly equal powers."

With Whitehurst's sermon ringing in their ears, the AP Chief and his cameraman set about getting more footage for studio editing and then they came upon the solitary figure of Rachael.

The covers of Time and People magazines, both had the black and white images of Rachael, her hair a bit disheveled, wisps and tufts of hair obscuring her porcelain face, making her a seductive beauty, wearing combat fatigues, a bullet proof vest with "Police" in bold lettering, as she stood vigil over the twisted rubble where a comrade had given his own life to save her and the others. The single tear line down her cheek was commented on by the President speaking to congress about the budget proposed for law enforcement and the dedicated service they perform each day.

Rachael's mournful image became a symbol for women everywhere, as a claim was made that a woman can be a combat soldier, ready to defend this country or arrest murders, yet frail enough to cry at the losses that are sure to follow.

For her bravery and courage in the face of death and destruction, Rachael was awarded the Medal of Freedom from the President of the United States, who flew to Chicago for the presentation and ensuing dinner party where she and Daniel Salvino were welcomed by the dignitaries and millionaires'.

What the public never learned, however, is that Rachel had entombed the President's award in a plastic capsule and while Gibson's grave was still freshly mounded, had buried it as her private tribute to the man she once detested.

Daniel was present as her security and safe haven from the prying eyes that dared not interfere.

Chapter 29

"Special Agent Melvin Gibson, affectionately called 'Hollywood' by his co-workers, was buried today, here in Chicago where he recently moved," the commentator said softly, as footage taken earlier that day were shown in the background.

In a mile long procession of officers from every department in the State of Illinois, along with hundreds of FBI agents and employees, followed the horse drawn caisson carrying the American flag draped casket that carried sandbags and a photograph taken from Gibson's employment file. The unique sound of a hundred plus bagpipes filled the air, custom that is reserved to fallen Chicago police officers and firefighters who gave their lives in the line of duty, was extended to Gibson at the direction of the Mayor himself.

Members of the teams, who accompanied Gibson that fateful night, were his honor guard and walked on each side of the bronze casket. Wearing the gear they wore that night, was a tribute to a solider and a few members' still sported bandages covering their burns from the flash. The streets were lined with grateful citizens, who saluted Gibson as he was carried past, or flowers were tossed towards the carriage by mourners who cried at his loss.

Rachael led the Chicago contingent, while Khoren lead the FBI people on the opposite side. Although she was the celebrity and one of the most sought after women in America by the media, she shunned all calls or references to her by the on-lookers they passed on their way to the gravesite. For this solitary day, Sergeant Rachael Hart, was a soldier, a veteran in her own right and representing all those who stand between murderers and those they protect. Once again, a rogue tear escaped her eye and tricked down her cheek and once again, that image graced the covers of several national and international magazines covers, substantiating the ability to serve, while possessing the feminine quality of the ability and grace to cry openly.

Calvin Gillings and Ben Ori shared the limo that leads the vehicular entourage. Both men were to give gravesite eulogies, honoring a man who lost his life in the service of the Bureau and a hero who sacrificed all in order to save Chicago police officers.

At the end of the day, as the empty casket which symbolically represented the man, whose human remains were never found or forensically identified by DNA, was lowered into the earth, while a twenty one gun salute was fired overhead, everyone present felt the presence of the renegade agent called "Hollywood."

In death, Melvin Gibson cemented a relationship between the FBI and the Chicago Police Department, which brought cooperation and communication that was previously lacking. Even the President sent the First Lady as his emissary, with condolences from a grateful nation.

Chapter 30

While Gibson's burial was national news and dominated the media, there was an antithetical ceremony taking place at a small gathering in Wheaton, where immediate family, the neurosurgeon and a few friends, gathered to mourn the loss of Evan Felder.

As his wife attested, Evan suffered from a medical condition so heinous, that he no longer had control of his thought processes and was slain by the cops, in a senseless display of brute force and the desire to employ lethal force, even on the infirm.

The media refused to attend, as to do so, would run afoul of all precedent in such situations. Posing the Mantis as some martyr, would be tantamount to suicide and the horrible end to any media career.

Evan Felder had no gravesite ceremony or grave which would be desecrated for ages to come or become a shrine to the macabre.

Even Felder just ceased to exist.

Chapter 31

"Sergeant Hart?" the caller asked.

"Yes, who is this? I don't do interviews or appearances on any talk shows. If you're... was all she said before being interrupted.

"This is Whitehurst from the FBI Crime Lab in Washington. Remember me?"

"I remember Mr. Whitehurst. How do I know this is the same person?" she asked.

"I handed you a key-fob, miniature badge, with Gibson's number on it. You still have it?" the caller said.

As a matter of fact, at that very moment, the key-fob badge rested on her desk as she silently grieved the loss of the man it represented.

"What can I do for you, Mr. Whitehurst?" she asked.

"I have to tell you something that will not appear on any report. Sort of like Waco, if you know what I mean?" he replied.

"What does that mean?" she asked him with a concerned note.

"Remember the waist trimmer belt with the pipe bombs that Gibson described as being wrapped around the gas line?"

"Sure, I saw it too. What about it?"

"It's lying on my desk here. It's charred and disarmed now, but it resembles what Gibson described on the radio." He said flatly.

"so, if the belt didn't explode and set off the whole mess, what did?"

"We have no trace elements of any explosive materials whatsoever and the gas company said that the gas lines were not ruptured, but melted the valves, which sealed gas inside and away from the fire." Whitehurst explained.

"So, what happened? What claimed Gibson and Felder, Mr. Whitehurst? You're the expert here." She replied.

After a long pause, he answered. "If I were asked that question in my professional capacity, I'd say that the origin is unidentified at the present time."

"And your real feelings on this?" she asked.

"I'd say that hell paid us a little visit."

Epilog

The Mantis lives in all of us. He is the measuring rod for good and evil.

The Bible speaks of the Dark Lord, Satan or Lucifer or even the serpent, but in any event, memorializes His existence as surely as there is a God.

Do you believe?

daniel

Daniel Storm

Mr. Storm is Native American and ascribes to the Blackfoot heritage and ways. He grew up in Illinois and Wisconsin, where he attended the University of Wisconsin and ultimately studied law. After college, he participated in defending some of America's most notable crime figures, while associated with prestigious law firms.

As an author of numerous crime/fiction novels, he spends hours creating stories that compel readers to devote their undivided attention. Internationally, he is on the threshold of tremendous success, despite his retaining control of his stories, the production of his books and distribution.

He lives near Milwaukee with his German Shepherd, Merlin. He enjoys seeing the sites in Wisconsin on his Harley.

As a Viet Nam veteran, Storm works within the Wisconsin community to assist soldiers and military families, both of those in active service, and veterans and their families.

www.danielstormauthor.com

www.ingramcontent.com/pod-product-compliance
Lightning Source LLC
Chambersburg PA
CBHW061154170626
46809CB00003B/1091